Hope Never Knew Horizon

DOUGLAS BRUTON

TAPROOT PRESS

First published by Taproot Press 2024

ISBN: 978-1739207786

Printed and bound by

Typeset in 11.5 point Garamond by
Main Point Books, Edinburgh

Cover design: Anna Morrison

'A Promise is firmer than a Hope, although it does not hold so much – Hope never knew Horizon'

(from a poem/letter sent by Emily Dickinson to her sister-in-law, Susan Huntington Dickinson)

THE WEXFORD WHALE (i)

Ned Wickham and I don't ever believe a word that comes out of his mouth. He said I was pretty as sunrises once but then the next day I saw him kissing Brid by the shore and he had a posy of flowers that he presented to her. He said one day we'd be joined together in the church and in front of God and that was a year ago and maybe Brid has changed his mind for he has said nothing of it since. And sometimes Ned has a drink in him, which is not but what all men do, and then he talks pretty and all his whisky-words slopping like water in a full-to-the-brim bucket when it's carried up steps. And he says also that he has more than twenty pounds in the bank but he still lives with his mam.

Then on this March morning, when he's back from his shift at the lifeboat, he comes a knocking at my door and he says when I open it that now we are made and he scoops me up in his arms and dances me across the road, me in my slippers and housecoat and my hair not brushed so that anyone watching must think me a poor and common slattern.

'Made is it?' I say. 'When you haven't two pennies to rub together, Ned Wickham.'

'Ah but now,' he says and taps one finger along the bridge of his nose and by that I am to believe he has something up his sleeve, like a rabbit that's pulled out of a hat or doves that suddenly appear from the folds of a handkerchief.

'Put me down, Ned Wickham. I am not yours to be carrying around like a pebble you picked up off the beach.'

Then he tells me he's found a whale, as though a whale might be as easily lost as a penny ha'penny. And like I said, he is just not to be believed, not a single word.

'Oh, but a great hill of a whale and it's just lying there kicking its tail in the shallows beyond the harbour. And it has my name on it now, Kitty, which makes it mine. We have been out to see it, me and Blake and Saunders. Rowed out to introduce us-selves and to look into the wet of its great staring eye.'

Maybe I rolled my eyes or sighed or made a sound in the back of my throat, something that told Ned Wickham that I did not believe him, any more than I believed him when he said he once ate a whole roast pig and he could not move from his bed for three days and was why he'd missed our date to go dancing; or when he said he had floated off the ground, all with the power of his mind, and he was light as a feather then and the wind carried him from Rosslare Point to Raven Point in the blink of an eye.

'Hand on my heart, Kitty, I speak no word of a lie.'

'A whale is it now. And what good is a whale with the name of Ned Wickham on it, except that the story might get you a drink in the Wexford Arms of a Saturday night when the men there are a wee bittie deeper in their cups and for that a little looser with their wits and their money?'

He sets me on my feet, crooks his arm and offers his elbow for me to slip my hand into, like we're a couple at a fancy do.

'There's money in a whale,' he says then.

'Just like there's money in a bank?'

'Not just twenty-pounds,' says Ned. 'Maybe a hundred, or we can hope for a hundred and twenty.'

And like that he's floating off the ground again.

'Get your coat and your boots and we'll go see,' he says, and he won't take no for an answer and he says if I don't come see, he'll ask Brid by the shore to come in my place.

Ah, but Ned Wickham knows which cards to play, and so I put my boots on and my coat and I go with him down towards the harbour, but I don't take his arm, not though he offers me it again and he's grinning like the cat that's got the best of the milk and he's breathing fast as steam trains.

And well enough there's a whale, just where he said it'd be, lying on its side, and it's in some distress and thrashing the water to foam with its tail and I says to Ned how it's a crying shame to see any animal so in pain. Ned nods and he says there's nothing he can do for it and all that beating of the tail will only make the whale stick faster on the mudbank and it won't ever be swimming in the open sea again and so it might as well fill up his pockets as any other's.

'If it was a horse and it was in such distress, you'd take a gun to its head and shoot it, Ned Wickham. The same for a dog or a mauled rabbit. Or a mole that the cat has been at and it has ripped the mole open, head to toe, so all its innards are spilling out and the cat has brought it as a gift for you and there's only mercy in killing that squealing mole, quick as a lick.'

Ned Wickham recalls hitting that mole with the flat blade of his spade, hitting it so hard it was quiet and dead in an instant and all because I asked him to.

'Do something, Ned Wickham, or I shall think you a Godless man and hard-hearted.'

*

All through the night the whale fought for its life. You could hear it moaning, like the wind in a night-gale, and it gasped for breath and slapped its tail down on the muddied water and shifted not a jot from its place out of the sea and on the cruel land.

Then in the full-moon early morning Ned Wickham and several men rowed out to the tired and weakened whale armed with metal rods and knives and wood-chopping axes. When they reached the whale, they clambered out of the boat and scaled the hill of blubber and set about beating the animal to death. The whale let out a cry of anguish and maybe it wept for a tear did seem to fall from its glassy eye – in Ned Wickham's retelling at least. And maybe Ned Wickham found God again in that moment, for he quickly fashioned a crude harpoon from a long blade and a metal bar and he plunged this makeshift spear under the whale's pectoral flipper and into its heart and so dispatched it at once. The blood turned the waters red and the cries of the gulls filled the air with such a screaming grief.

*

'Oh Ned,' I says to him when he is supping milky tea with two sugars from a tin cup at the table in my kitchen the next morning. He smells of fish and sweat and the sea. 'The hardest hurt is more easily borne when it is what God would have wished.' I stroke his wet hair from his face and kiss his cold salted cheek.

'I think it's maybe 80 foot long, the whale, maybe 90. It will have to be measured for the record. It will be in the newspaper and I am to give my side of the story to a reporter and they want to take my photograph. And that, Kitty, is the just the start.'

And that's so like Ned, counting his chickens as the saying goes. For the word out there is that the whale don't belong to Ned Wickham at all, nor ever could, for it belongs to the Crown, which is to say the whale is Queen Victoria's property and no one can take the 'Fish Royal' from her.

*

That Saturday and Easter Sunday the Wexford boatmen make a penny or two that the Queen can't touch ferrying sightseers out to take a closer look at the dead whale. It has by this time been identified as a female blue whale. She has begun to smell at this point so the ladies hold linen kerchiefs to their pinched noses and one man retches and is sick overboard. Still the boatmen's pockets are a good deal fuller after that weekend.

Behind the scenes there is some discussion on what's to be done with the Queen's property. And nine days after the death of the whale the carcass is sold at auction for £111. Ned Wickham is paid £50 for his part in the salvage of the whale and the story appears in the newspapers both in Ireland and in England.

*

When Ned Wickham is deeper in his cups than any man has a right to be, he tells the story of the Wexford Whale and like I said before he is not ever to believed. In the weeks and months after, the story grows arms and legs and runs crazy through the streets, hollering with its arms waving above its head. Ned tells how he single-handedly wrestled the whale into submission, up to his knees in the briny, and then took its life with all the heroism fitting of a sabre-wielding cavalryman at the Battle of Waterloo.

'It was like I was fighting Napoleon himself and I looked into the blood-in-its-eye of that great leviathan and I thrust my lance into the heart of the beast, so deep I was up to my armpits in gore.'

'That's not quite what it said in the newspaper,' says one of the men at the bar.

'Damn to hell all reporters, for they lie and only tell it like they want to tell it and they make each story toothsome to their readers, clipping and cutting till the story is only pretty and it won't make a gentle lady gasp for breath. Up to my armpits in gore I say.'

And all Ned Wickham's spittle-words slap against the walls of the Wexford Arms like the sea in a breached harbour, and they fall back on Ned Wickham and wash over him, and soon enough he slumps in his chair and falls into sleep. And if you lean into the sleeping drunk and listen sharp as pins, you can sometimes still hear the man talking, all his words sluiced and slopping, and the one story spilling from Ned Wickham's lips over and over, a story to drink out on for the rest of his days.

'We are made,' is what he said on that first March morning that he sighted the whale, but I do not think £50 is enough to make any man for we still have not been to church to take our vows before God and I am beginning to think we never shall. Besides, Ned Wickham is these days so often in the drink – by which I do not mean the sea for that would be perfectly normal for the coxswain of the Wexford lifeboat – no, he is so often drunk that I am not sure that he is the man I fell in love with, nor ever will be again.

When I see Brid by the shore, I take her hand soft in mine and I tell her in earnest that she is welcome to him, but I am not sure she doesn't feel the same as I do.

EMILIE, EMILY, E (i)

Sure but Miss Emily thinks no one knows. She thinks she has something that's a tidy secret, like a flower pressed neat between the pages of a book and that book sitting on a library shelf somewhere and so many books in that library that the pressed flower cannot be found. 'Cept I discovered that pressed flower, see, and now she is found out.

It was washday Monday in Amherst, same as every Monday, and she knew to pass her dresses and underclothes down to me and her sheets and pillowcases too, all done the night before or not washed till next Monday. Everyone in the house knew. I'd been up since early doors, creeping like shadows or mice. Even before the bread was to be baked in the oven, the water was on to boil in the copper and all the house but me asleep and the smell of Sunlight soap thickening the air, thick as three-day-old soup and catching in the back of my mouth so I was clearing my throat with every second breath.

Course I had my suspicions before then. Miss Emily was all

lit up some days, see, and others she was dull as dark mornings or slamming the door to her room so hard I feared for the hinges; and I thought I had the reason for all that, a wee idea anyways, but what I found confirmed it.

She writes letters, don't she now, everyone knows that. It's her way of being in the world without venturing forth. Her fingers is always stained with ink and once the sleeve of her blouse was so blue on the cuff that it took for me to soak it in lye to lift it. And poems she writes – she keeps them in her desk drawer and a lock on that drawer so no one can see in, especially not her father. 'A woman should keep her thoughts on more domestic concerns,' is what he would say, each word given a certain emphasis with the wag of his finger. Mostly Miss Emily's careful, but one day she was not and I saw the little books of poetry all stacked neat and numbered. Din't mean much to me when I read one of her poems, but that's no nevermind.

Letters and poetry, and books with small writing in the margins. And if there's no paper by she writes on the corner of the bedsheet or sometimes on the wall, low down and behind a table or chair so it might not be seen. 'Cept I seen it. Just a word sometimes or a name, the one name over and over and over.

Well then now, this washday Monday morning and I was sorting through the clothes and the bedsheets. Some can take a hard boiling and some need the water not so hot. And the whites should not be mixed with the coloureds for clothes bleed as easy as pricked thumbs. I have an order to everything, an order arrived at with the years I've been doing the washing for the house. Sheets and pillowcases first and a great wooden dollie-stick to stir them in the maidening-tub; then the lighter coloured clothes, and last of all the darker dresses. I sorts them into three piles and that way I know how the day will unfold.

About six – and I always knows it's six by the ringing of the church bells – I had the bread punched down for its second rise and the kitchen oven was fed with wood so it'd be hot for baking by seven, and the water in the copper was bubbling hard and so I could begin. I had a girl that helped me once but she was a thin slip of a thing and she complained about the work and how her arms ached with the turning of the dollie-stick and she was sticky with sweat from the heat in the wash-house and her hair came undone from the pins and fell across her face like the tails of mice or rats. Now I do it all myself.

Like I said before, sheets and pillowcases first and you've got to beat that dollie-stick till the breath in you is short and quick and the strings in your arms is tight as stretched wet rope and your back is pinching across the shoulders. Then everything plunged into a rinsing tub and the water in there is cold as though it's been pulled fresh from the well and it numbs the fingers and chills the bones.

I wrings the water from the sheets by twisting. Maybe one day soon the house will purchase one of those new 'wringers' and that'd make it all a bit easier, but I manage. And when the sheets are all shook and pegged out on the line and the air is blowing hard as punches and kicks, then I can turn to the blouses and dresses and the stockings and ladies' undergarments.

So, I was going through the dresses see. Some of them is very pretty and no one is ever by in the washhouse so I sometimes holds them against me and I imagine what it is to be Miss Emily or the Mistress. That's when I found it and it was good that I did for Miss Emily would have been all cat claws and spitting if it had been lost to the washing. I dipped my hand into one of Miss Emily's dress pockets. To be sure there was no mischief in what I did, I was just fancying what it was to be a woman with time to write letters and poetry, or just to stand and stare at the birds singing in the trees for above an hour – I saw Miss Emily do that once, a whole idle hour. And she stood with her hands in the pockets of her dress and so I was wondering what that would be like.

Pinned in the pocket of Miss Emily's dress was a letter, pinned so it never could be lost, though had it been put through the washing and beaten with the dollie-stick a hundred times till the water ran clean, there would not have been much of a letter left after that.

I unpinned it and took it out from Miss Emily's dress pocket. It was not sealed or yet addressed but only folded and pinned and so I thought it nothing more than a poem she might have written or a recipe copied down from a book or a note on what she needed from the stationer's – new paper or ink or pens. And where's the harm in looking to see what she'd written if she'd written only that?

Only it was a wee letter and I know I should not have read it, should have folded it shut again and set the pin back in place and delivered it back to Miss Emily.

'Dear and dearest' is how it began and more than that, 'Darling' and other such endearments. On and on it went about how Miss Emily missed this person she was writing to, how the days when she din't hear from them were long and every hour had in it a hundred hours and Miss Emily could not bear it, that time weighed so heavy. I do not have the letter to heart so I only remember and memory is ever imperfect so I only recall the sense of what was written. But one line I do have and Miss Emily wrote 'I begin to hope for you', by which I believe she meant that she hoped her love would be returned pound for pound.

It was a love letter. It was the loveliest love letter I ever saw and I was a little out of breath with the reading of it and I think maybe that was the intent. Breathless and light-headed I was so that I had to sit, there on the washroom floor. Oh, if only I was loved like that, I thought, and I pressed that thought and the letter to my heart.

After, I folded the letter and pinned it fast and set it where the hot air of the washroom could not reach and ruffle the page.

Later, when the bread was baked and set to cool and dresses danced on the drying line – and it is odd to me remembering that they danced that morning when they had not danced on any other washday Monday morning, or at least I had not ever thought of them as dancing before – and the house was up and about its business, I crept upstairs and quietly left the pinned letter on Miss Emily's desk.

I felt something then, when I closed the door of Miss Emily's room and the last that I saw of the letter was its place in the centre of her desk. I wasn't sure at first but it was as though the words of the letter were somehow mine, that I had written them and now awaited an answer, longed for a word of reply and some return for the love I had written. And I understood in that moment all Miss Emily's slammed shut doors and the stamped feet, and the sighing heard through open windows, or keyhole tears once. And the looking for the postboy each morning and asking and asking if he has yet been and if there was anything with her name on it.

I sighed and returned to the kitchen.

'Open me carefully,' Miss Emily'd written at the bottom of the page. And the letter was to Susan Huntington, 'Dear and darling Susie,' she'd wrote. And 'open me carefully' and not when anyone is by so that it is a secret just between Miss Emily and Miss Susan, 'cept now I know and my heart yearns and I look for the postboy now, as much as Miss Emily does, and I wonder where on earth he can be with his dillying and dallying, and I am a little cross when he does turn up and there is nothing for Miss Emily.

ADA ALICE PULLEN (i)

Men's hearts are so easily won. Just a carefully timed dip of my head, a look that holds his and then lets it go again and a way of shaping the mouth so the lips almost make one half of a kiss, needing only his lips to complete the act.

I don't know if that is quite how I won Sir's heart – he was always 'Sir', even when he held me to him and he said I was peaches and cream and he said he loved me to all the stars and back again; at least I once imagined him saying all that and he was still 'Sir' when he did. I had spent the day modelling for an artist in a studio in Kensington Green. It was good enough money for a fatherless girl with four sisters to feed and only one pair of shoes to her name, but I thought I could do better. The artist had said we should take a break and so I was at the door to the studio and just where the sun falls full at that hour of the day. I think I saw him before he saw me and maybe then I dipped my head and caught his eye and made soft kiss-shapes with my lips.

He stopped and introduced himself. He was an artist too and he was looking for a model for a painting he had in mind and he thought I might serve him well in this regard. Those are his words and not mine. He gave me his card and said I should call him the next day. He may have mentioned a price for the day, but I'm not sure I recall what it was.

Sir was old enough he could have been my father but that didn't seem to concern him. He already had the title for the painting and in his head an idea of how it would be. He had procured a dress that was fitting for that idea – an old dress, white with black ribbon, and the sleeves puffed and ruffled like feathers. He said I could change into the dress behind a screen that was in one corner of his studio.

Then he positioned me where the light was to his liking and in front of a hanging curtain in russets and golds. He fussed over the dress, adjusting it to his preferred lie and I felt the back of his hand brush against my breast and he snatched for breath then – I am sure that was how it was.

Then Sir stood back and sighed.

He pulled up a high chair and for the longest time just sat and looked. I could feel his eyes on me. I did not fidget – for artists do detest that – but held the pose. He said I was the most beautiful and he said looking at me he had so many pictures in his head and he said this would just be the start.

He took up a pencil and paper and began sketching.

'Tell me about yourself,' he said when he had finished.

I was about to move towards him to see what he had caught of me on the paper, but Sir pushed me back and said to stand as I had before and not to move except to say something about who I was.

He remained at a short distance and continued with his looking.

'I'm Ada Alice Pullen. I stay in a apartment in South Kensington wiv me four sisters. I'm a actress on the stage and sometimes a artist's model. I share a bed wiv one of me sisters and her breath smells of onions and she kicks her feet in her sleep and I'm all bruises below the knee. I'm 22 years old, if me mother is to be believed, which she almost never is.'

I'm not sure Sir liked the sound of my voice for his face creased and he seemed as one pricked with pins when I said certain words.

'An actress on the stage. I hope you speak the lines that others have written with less drawl and more shape to the words.'

Then Sir got to his feet, set his sketch aside, and approached where I stood. I had already made the mistake of moving so this time I did not. He leaned towards me and breathed in, as though I was a flower he was testing the scent of. Then he kissed my cheek and he said, 'Like that, quiet as empty churches, I can think my heart lost to your beauty.'

There must have been more to that first day than this but that is all memory allows me.

Maybe at the end I said that I hoped Sir was pleased and that he might ask me to model for the painting proper and I asked how many days that would involve and, if he paid by the day, how much that might be.

He sent for tea at the end of that first day – he must have done for he did the same every day that I modelled for him. He pulled a low table from the wall, arranged two high-backed armchairs facing each other and gestured for me to sit. Then when the maid delivered a tray with the tea things carefully arranged on it he waved her away and said he would manage without her.

He asked me if I took milk in my tea, and sugar, then he lifted the teapot and poured. I never saw the like before – a gentleman pouring tea for a scrap of a young woman like me.

The cups were a fine bone china made by Foley. They were gold lipped with fancy curlicue handles and delicate blue and pink flowers on the cream coloured bowls and scalloped gold rimmed saucers to stand in and silver spoons to stir the tea with.

Then he said a word. Just one word and it had no context

and so seemed out of place. He said simply 'south' and asked me to repeat it back to him. I did as he asked and he then said I wasn't saying it right and scolded me and told me to listen. He said it again and he told me to repeat it. I did.

'No, no, no. There is no 'f' at the end of the word.'

And he said it again, exaggerating each part of the word and ending with his tongue between his teeth.

I said it back to him and he nodded.

'Better,' he said. 'Practice that for the next time.'

'What, like 'omework?'

He laughed and shook his head.

And so began Sir's lessons on how I should better speak.

'Bring me a script you are working on and we can go through it together.'

I sipped at my tea and considered the whole arrangement.

'You won't be charging me for the lessons on how to talk?'

Then he got up from his chair and walked to a small chest of drawers. From the top drawer he took out a small hinged box the size of a carrot. He placed it on the table in front of me.

'I hope I am not being too forward in gifting this to you. Think of it as a small inducement to return.'

It was a necklace, a fine chain in either brass or gold. And hanging from the chain was a single pearl the size of a small pea. I feel in writing all this down I am overusing vegetables in describing this first piece of jewellery that Sir gave to me. He offered to put it around my neck and to fasten the clasp at the back. He had to lift the loose hair on my neck and I think he rather liked that.

'Ada Alice Pullen – we may have to do something with that,' he said.

I did not know what he meant.

THE WEXFORD WHALE (ii)

There was a bit of a buzz in the auction house that day, I can tell you, and some of the people there came from far off and spoke with clipped tongues and they did not know the manners of Wexford, which may be particular and not London-manners. They were dressed smart and they smelled of cinnamon and nutmeg, or something spiced at least, and they smoked fancy clay pipes with rich scented tobacco, and gold watch chains hung heavy from their waistcoat pockets and they were always checking to see how many minutes had passed and they frowned more and more at their watch faces, growing impatient at the Wexford way of starting when the day has had a chance to catch its breath.

A bell was rung to begin the proceedings and the auctioneer, a man I knew well, stood a little taller that day as though with so many gentlemen in the room his importance was increased. He gave a brief description of the Fish Royal and the circumstances of its discovery. It was a female blue whale and it measured 82 feet in length – something shorter than the brag of Ned Wickham – and it lay on a mudbank just beyond the harbour. To be sure he might have given an estimate to its weight, I don't fully recall.

As chairman of the Wexford Harbour Board the matter of the blue whale lying in close proximity to the harbour was of some consequence to me. Besides, I thought privately there might be money in a blue whale if the price that day was right and not inflated by the gentlemen in the room. I am, see, a man of business.

In the end it was neither one thing nor another. The gentlemen from London were more white-faced than I had at first noticed, from the boat-crossing perhaps which the day before had been blowy, the sea all swollen and chopped. And the rooms they'd taken at the Wexford Arms were not so fine as they were used to and the beds not so soft so maybe they had been tossed and turned out of their sleep. To be sure the whale went for more than I had wanted to pay but not beyond the limit I had set myself and so I was pleased enough to get her for £111.

The crown had to pay Ned Wickham for his finding of the whale, though anyone walking the shore that morning in March would have found it if he had not. It was a whale after all and it was where a whale was not wont to be.

I immediately took into my employ some 20 local men and gave instructions for the cutting up of the meat of that no-more Fish Royal. It was not fit food for man or woman, I understood that, but I reckoned on making something by selling it off as food for dogs. And I made arrangements for the blubber to be boiled so that the oil might be extracted and stored in 45 gallon wooden barrels until it could be sold.

'How many barrels?' said Cooty the Cooper.

He was as much a man of business as I was and looking to make a penny or two for himself from the blue whale.

I told Cooty that I didn't want barrels I couldn't use and so I'd start with ten and only need more if they were filled.

'Might be as many as fifteen or twenty barrels in her, do you think?' I said.

He had no more idea than I had for we had neither of us dealt in whales before.

I calculated what might be the return on all of this, wrote the figures down in two uncertain columns, the outgoings and the income, and was content that a small profit was promised even after the men had been paid.

Being a blue whale there was also the baleen to be sold for I knew there was a demand for that stiff bone-like material. My own shirt collars kept their shape from the baleen inserted under the fabric and Mrs Armstrong got her own thin waist from the whalebone corsets she wore under her dresses.

'And will there be a pretty penny or two from the sale of your whale, as many pretty pennies as would buy a woman a new Sunday dress perhaps?'

Mrs Armstrong had more dresses than could be worn in a week of Sundays and I did not see the need for yet another and so I said we would have to see. There were pennies to come in and pennies to go out and I was not yet certain that all costs would be covered.

I had a backscratcher made of baleen also and so I thought to make a penny or two from the sale of the blue whale's baleen.

All just business.

Then I read something in the newspaper, something about a museum in London that was given over to natural history and something that the Naturalist Darwin said about where we came from as a species, which was from apes. I didn't think this so big a conclusion to have arrived at, for there are, I think, men in Wexford who are in appearance and habit closer to apes than they are to men. But that's not what caught my attention in the newspaper article. No indeed. The article gave some description of the contents of the museum and the animal skeletons on show, great bears from America and something called a hippopotamus from Africa and even the full skeleton of an elephant from India. This last was the museum's boast and it made particular reference to the size of the elephant skeleton and how it would take the breath away of any visitor to the museum. And so it occurred to me that the complete skeleton of an 82-foot-long blue whale might be a greater attraction.

I wrote to the museum and told them I had such for sale, a complete blue whale skeleton, and for a good enough price I would arrange for its delivery to the museum.

By return I received a letter on headed paper from a person who had been instructed to open negotiations for the whale skeleton, one Albert Günther acting on behalf of William Henry Flower, who was the then Director of the Natural History department of The British Museum. I had in my letter made so bold as to suggest a sale price of £250. Albert Günther protested in his letter that £250 was overdear and he instead made an offer of £200 for the complete skeleton and other parts of the whale that might be recovered such as the baleen.

Now might Mrs Armstrong have her new Sunday dress and I would not care a jot that it made a hole in my profits from the whale, for the profits would be enough and magnified by the sale of its skeleton and so in the end the hole a dress might make was not to be thought such a great hole.

In the Wexford Arms that evening I bought Ned Wickham a drink, and then another, and I put my arm across his shoulders and said how he was a man of distinction in the town and I would buy him a drink every Saturday for a year on account of the finding of that blue whale.

I confess I was a little giddy from the letter I'd received from the museum. A man should not conduct business when he is so giddy, not even Saturday night business in the Wexford Arms. Ned Wickham was, to be sure, drunk enough that Saturday that I hope not to be held to my promise.

The skeleton of the blue whale had to be boiled so all the flesh and muscle fell easy from the bone and only when the bones were clean and polished white as Greek marble could they be boxed up and made ready for their transportation across the sea to London, England. I had a man make a drawing of the whale and the 252 bones of its skeleton so that the once Fish Royal might be put back together when it was located in its new home.

Then I sat down at my desk and busied myself with addition and subtraction to come near to a final tally of the money that the blue whale had brought me.

EMILIE, EMILY, E (ii)

Ach, but the young think they have a monopoly on love. They look at a person of my years and think we never could have loved, not like they love, not with such a passion. And so they think we do not, nor ever could, understand. Oh Miss Emily! I know!

Today a letter was delivered to the house and it was as though it was for me 'cept that it bore Miss Emily's name. I took it from the postboy and patted his arm and said he had made a woman happier than he could ever know. He might have thought that woman was Miss Emily and to be sure it was; but I was also made happy by its arrival for I had looked for it just as much.

I held it to me, pressed to my chest and breathed in deep. Then I turned it over and over in my hands as if the words inside could be discerned by a closer inspection of the outside. Then to my ear as if what Miss Susan Huntington had written could be heard whispering through the seal of the envelope.

If I delayed in passing the letter on to Miss Emily it was only briefly and only so I might have something of that love to myself a while. The young think women of my years also do not want for love but want just for a full stomach and an easy Sunday. It is not so.

Did Miss Emily's hand tremble when I passed the letter from my hand into hers? Was there a catch in her breath, a small gasp of surprise? Did she betray herself in any innocent way or was it only under my closer scrutiny that I saw what she thought to hide and anyone else being by would not have seen? Miss Emily was in rapture.

'I should like to take tea in my room,' she said in an effort to control her emotions, but there was a shake in her voice, that much was certain. Dear Miss Emily, I know!

I understood that she wanted to be alone and comfortable and to read over and over the words written by Miss Susan Huntington.

'I do begin to hope for you,' I said to myself as I closed the door of her room behind me and tripped light-footed down the stairs to make the tea.

On my return, some fifteen minutes later by the clock, was the air in the room somehow altered? Lighter maybe, scented with roses as though the outside had been let into the room. I placed the tea tray down on a low table and asked if that was all.

Miss Emily was distracted and at the same time lit up and I could see she was reading the letter in her hand, lost in the words, maybe for the second or third time, for that is what I would be doing if I was a woman of her tender years and had by me a letter from someone I loved so hard.

I snatched a look over Miss Emily's shoulder and caught only a few short words from Miss Susan Huntington. 'Oh dear Sister, what it is to love.' I think I might have let out a signal of *my* feelings then. A sigh perhaps, or a moan, or some small sound that revealed my own heart's yearning.

Miss Emily, suddenly aware that I had not left the room, thanked me for the tea and said that would be all, by which I knew I was to go.

I descended the stairs once more and made myself a cup of tea and sat at the kitchen table with my own thoughts of what might be in the letter that Miss Emily was even then lost in.

I had seen them together, see. Oh but it was a while back and before I had found the pinned letter in Miss Emily's dress pocket. Maybe it was last summer or the summer before. They were sitting on the grass in the garden and I overheard Miss Susan – Susie – remark on the birdsong that was spinning on the air.

'It is a linnet, I do believe,' Miss Emily had said.

And they held hands then as though the song of that linnet

was the greatest wonder of the known world and they were the only witnesses to it. And oh, the way Miss Emily held Miss Susan's hand, as if it was made of glass and might break with too firm a hold and like that her hand was nothing more than a gentle nest for Miss Susan's small hand to rest in. That were enough, if I had known what I know now, but I do think I also remember the look on Miss Emily's face, maybe I do, and it was the look I have seen on the faces of saints in church books and in paintings on the walls of the vestry and once I saw the same look carved in white stone and the stony Saint Teresa did seem to breathe and sigh in ecstasy. But sure now, I think I am adding to the memory with that discovered 'I do begin to hope for you' and that 'Oh dear Sister, what it is to love.'

I lifted the teacup to my kissing lips – see how I am: my lips to the cup lip are kissing lips and they never were that before. I sipped at the tea, let its wet sweet warmth sit on my tongue before swallowing. And I thought then of a person I'd once loved and he had loved me and it was so many years back that it was as though that love belonged to someone else and was not a memory harboured in my own heart. And I wondered where he was now, that soft-spoken man with his quick hands, quick as mice under my dress. I placed my hand where my heart is and in memory it was his hand.

Oh Miss Emily, to be sure women of my years have loved

and lost and still want for love, and know what it is to be heartsore and filled up both at the same time. To be sure Miss Emily, we know!

Later in the morning, I returned to Miss Emily's room on the pretext of collecting the tea tray. I knocked on her door, not hard as hammers nor so soft as birdwing, but something that I hoped was gentle at least. There was no reply and so I thought Miss Emily must be about somewhere, in the garden perhaps, or in the library or with her mother. I turned the handle and pushed my way into the room.

She was asleep on the bed, still in her dress so that my first thought was on the creases that would need pressed out of the cloth of her dress with a stove-hot iron and a wet napkin. But then on tip-toe like a dancer – which for a woman of my years is something to be wondered at – I drew a little closer to the sleeping Miss Emily. It must be said that the young woman was a plain woman and she did not make the most of what she had, her hair and the clothes that she chose to wear and the way she sat in a chair sometimes. In her hand she still held the letter that the postboy had delivered that morning and on her sleeping face was a smile that made her look pretty – yes now, pretty is it! And that is what love can do when it has two sides, the loving and the beloved, like a two headed coin and the one side is the same as the other.

I lifted the tea tray, careful not to rattle the teacup in its saucer, and quietly left Miss Emily's room and returned to the work that waited me below stairs.

I never did see that letter again and must suppose that once it was answered it was folded shut again and put with the poems and the other letters from Miss Susan Huntington in the locked drawer of Miss Emily's desk. But that is not to say that I din't think of it often and compose in my thoughts a reply that was full of kissing lips and linnets singing and hands on hearts.

'Please to see that this letter is taken straightway to the post,' said Miss Emily the very next morning.

I said I would take it myself, and if I tarried a little on the walk to the post office it was only so that I could hold love in my hand and not so easily let it go, as I had when I was young and foolish enough not to know what it was to have such a love nor what it was to lose it and to miss it ever after.

The letter was addressed to Miss Susan Huntington and from the pen-kick and curl of the letters in her name on the front of the envelope it was obvious – at least to me – what tender sentiments awaited inside.

ADA ALICE PULLEN (ii)

Sir took maybe a week to complete that first painting and though I say it myself, and if the painting is to be believed, I am indeed beautiful – which is to say I believe the painting. I was at the same time as sitting for him, rehearsing for a play. I do not think he wanted me to do this play. He had plans for me, he said. But I told him on this I was not to be swayed. I had a taste for it, I told him. He muttered into his beard and his words were all spit and grumble and he said I could do it only so long as it did not tire me out for he needed me pretty and fresh.

He was always clearing his throat, as though he had something important to say and clearing was to announce that, but clearing his throat was all that it was. He kept fussing over my dress, arranging the folds so that it looked right to his eye and so it said something about the girl beneath the dress – that's how he put it. He did this even when I was not posed for a painting but sitting with him taking tea and cake in front of his studio window with all the bright day looking in.

'I have another picture in mind,' he said.

I had won this gentle old man over, though he would not have been so fond to hear me call him 'old'. But there was already grey in his beard and the creases around his eyes spoke to the years of squinting to better see the paint on his brush and when he sat in a chair or got to his feet again he made a noise in the back of his throat as though sitting or standing required great physical effort.

'I have a friend in Ireland and he wants a picture for his home. There is a river runs through his property and I had a fancy to paint a water nymph. And that water nymph is you, my dear.'

He did not look at me when he spoke of the painting and so I thought there was more to this project than he was telling me.

'Do not say I'm to sit in cold water for day after day like the pretty Ophelia in her heavy dress and all flowers. I heard what she caught a dreadful chill and after she coughed like a old dog. Do not say, Sir, that I'm to sit in cold water.'

He laughed then but I was not warmed by his laughter and I looked at him a little more closely to see what it was that was still hidden.

He cleared his throat again and so I thought he might say without me prodding him. But again it was just the clearing of his throat. Then he got to his feet, and he made that sound that said it was an effort to do so. He paced the studio and looked thoughtful.

'What is it?' I said.

'It's just that…'

Then he left a space and did not seem in any hurry to fill it, not though I was hanging on his every word.

'It's just what?' I prompted.

He stopped his pacing and looked at me. I was used to the stab and pierce of that gaze so it did not trouble me.

'What?' I said again.

'It's a water nymph,' he said. Then he went to the far corner of the room and retrieved for my inspection a sketch he had made of how the painting would be.

I looked it over and still I could not see what it was that so troubled him.

The sketch showed a woman with her hands crossed just under her chin and her face dipped. She was naked except for a length of cloth that was draped down one side of her body and behind her water fell from a height above her head and in the drawing you could not tell what was falling cloth and what was falling water.

'Tell me I am to pose in the studio and not under some waterfall in the hills, cold and shivering and near to catching my death.'

'Her name is Crenaia,' he said. 'It's Greek.'

I shrugged and asked when he wanted to start and how long it might take and what payment I could expect.

'Then you will do it?' he said.

I do not think he expected that I would so easily agree. I think he thought the nakedness might be an obstacle to my posing for him and he did not know how to ask that of me. Maybe he'd had the idea for the picture before he met me, but I suspect the idea came after and it was a way for him to see me without my clothes. Men are, I think, not so complicated when all's said and done

Once terms had been agreed and a date set for the commencement of the work, I took my leave. He helped me on with my coat and I felt his breath hot on my cheek as he leaned into me.

Then I kissed him, just the lightest touch of my lips to his. He flushed a little and he snatched for breath and then cleared his throat and might have said something except no words came out of his mouth only sounds – sounds like the stammering of a fool. I have seen a landed fish before and it opened its mouth just the same.

Later, when I was going over and over the lines for my part in the play with a fellow actress keeping me to the words that were written down, she stopped me and said I was speaking different and not like I was used to speak. I told her about Sir and how he was teaching me to talk like a lady and how at the same time I was now to undress for him and to stand naked so he could run his eyes over every part of me.

'And he wants that I should change my name and not be Ada Alice Pullen but something prettier. "A rose by any other name would smell as sweet" is not a maxim that Sir holds to. I am inclined towards the name 'Dorothy'. What do you think? Could I be a Dorothy?'

'Like the poet's sister?'

'Like my own sister. She died.'

And that's how it came to be that I took my dead sister with me onto the stage, that she somehow lived again and I was mother to her, I hope a better mother than our own had been. I later explained this to my living sisters and there were tears in their eyes when they said my new name out loud – Dorothy.

The next time I was with Sir in his studio, and he said I could undress behind the screen and there was a diaphanous cloth that hardly hid the right side of my naked body and my left was all on show, I said to him that I thought I could live with the name 'Dorothy'.

He nodded – maybe at my naked body as much as at my suggestion. Then he cleared his throat and said my new name out loud. He was thoughtful for a moment before adding,

'Dorothy Pullen is still not quite right. Try Dorothy Dene. I think that has a ring to it.'

He was always talking rings, I thought, and I suspected he had plans for me there too.

'Dorothy Dene,' I said, testing the name on my tongue as though it was a new cake or a different flavour of tea. 'Yes, I like the sound of that and the taste. It slips easy off the tongue. I could live with that name. Dorothy Dene.'

He positioned me in front of a dark cloth. He said I should dip my head a little and hold my arms across my breasts, my hands crossed under my chin and my left leg just a half step in front of my right and with the weight shifted a little so my heel was not pressed to the floor and my left knee as though I might curtsey. He arranged the cloth over my right shoulder and down my back. And onto the floor.

'Dorothy Dene,' he said under his breath and he ran one hand down my left upper arm.

Then he retreated to behind his easel and quietly began work on the painting. It was something smaller than the last painting, something that could be smuggled into a house under wraps and the lady of the house not aware that it was there until it was placed on the wall of the gentleman's study in Ireland. A naked water nymph with a fancy Greek name to make her respectable.

'Dorothy Dene,' he said again.

THE WEXFORD WHALE (iii)

If I have, in my account of the sale of the whale and the stripping of the flesh from its bones and the boiling of those same bones, made it appear that all was plain sailing, then I have done wrong. In the end, not £200 was paid to William Armstrong for the whale skeleton but £150, and not sold direct to the museum or even to Albert Günther but to a further intermediary, Edward Gerrard Snr. There was some anxiety over the retrieval of the small vestigial pelvic bones that might so easily be lost and which were considered so important to science. Indeed, it took some time to locate these and for them to be safely 'harvested'.

Mr Edward Gerrard Snr was, as a skilled taxidermist, well placed to understand the articulation of the blue whale skeleton, and he must have travelled to Wexford and overseen the work being done for he sent regular reports to Albert Günther of the progress that was made.

The whole process was slow and it was the work of months.

It was May before the transportation of bones began, travelling across the Irish sea to Bristol and then across land to London. A full report was not completed for the British Museum until February of the following year. With transportation costs the final amount paid was £178.

There was great excitement in South Kensington as they took delivery of the blue whale skeleton. It would be something to shout about when it went on display and it was expected to draw sizeable crowds to the museum. But in 1892 that was a long way off. At 82 feet long and weighing in at three tons, there was no room large enough to house such a 'beast' and so the whale and all its parts was boxed up and put in storage, where it remained for more than forty years.

There was a museum assistant who worked there but his name is lost to the story so that it is as though he never existed at all. He was a smaller man than the others already named and in truth he had no part to play in the story of the whale. He read about its arrival in Kensington in his newspaper and it was specifically this that prompted him to apply for a post in the museum sometime that same year, the year that the blue whale was boxed up and stored out of sight.

Out of sight is not necessarily out of mind for there continued to be discussions down the years on how best to display the whale bones and calculations made on the cost and how it might be managed and drawings commissioned for a space grand enough to be home to the whale skeleton. And this nameless museum assistant, he kept a scrapbook of all that pertained to the whale, each time it was mentioned in the newspapers, the minutes of meetings where it was discussed and the photographs that leaked out which documented the journey from Ireland to Bristol and then to London and Kensington. And scribbled copies of the architect's drawings that changed from one year to the next.

Then at night, when all the city slept and this same museum assistant was charged with checking that the windows and doors were everywhere locked and no one was loitering in the corridors and the floors had been swept and all was quiet and still in the museum, he stole to the back of the building where the public were not to enter, and he walked among the storage boxes and his breath was held and he listened with a sharp ear – sharp as a butcher's knife he'd have said for his father had been a butcher – and he went in search of those boxes that held the bones of the blue whale.

And when he found them he put his ear to the boxes, pressed hard so he could hear the smallest sound inside.

Do not think for a moment that the bones in those boxes sat quiet and still. They shifted sometimes, and settled, and shifted again, restless in their dark dry nests; and there was always a sound that clung to them, stubborn and unshakeable. And if you asked that museum assistant what that sound was he would shrug and say it was like the shushing of the sea, the same that you hear when holding a seashell to the ear, and it was the kick and kick of water and a moaning sound, like music that is wayward and wordless and wild.

It was not known then that whales sing and that their magnificent songs carry across oceans, hopeful and full of yearning. But when that museum assistant wrote in his blue whale scrapbook, he made a record of what he heard and he described it as 'whale song'.

And when he was lying in his bed and in his own darkness, which was not box-darkness but street-light darkness and not really dark at all, he imagined he heard that whale song still, ringing in his ears.

He told only one other person and she asked if she could hear it too. Her name is also lost but she was real enough for this story. And he told her where to hide in the museum so that come closing time she would not be found. Then, when the lights were extinguished and he was doing his rounds, checking the windows and doors, picking up discarded tickets and sweet wrappers, he collected that young woman and hand in hand they went to the storage room and straight to the boxes where the whale skeleton was stored. Maybe they kissed, that is to be expected and so I do not make much of it here.

And he showed her how to press her cheek and her ear to one box after another and to hold her breath and her heartbeats so she could better hear. And after she said it was a wonder and she promised she'd heard it too and there in the dark of the storeroom she sang the same song back to the boxed whale, like an answer to its song, like a Litany prayer sung in church.

Do not ask me how I know this story and yet do not know the names of the museum assistant or the young woman. I can say only that I too have heard the whale bones singing, for the song never ends but rings down the ages. All you have to do is listen.

EMILIE, EMILY, E (iii)

Isn't it now also a madness? Sure and it's love I mean when I say that. And it stands the whole world on its head sometimes and one day is up and the next is down and nothing in those days to say which it will be. Like a child's swing and with the kick of her legs it lifts a small girl into the air only to let her fall again when it is at its highest point. The same is it with love – madness.

And no letter today or for a week now, no letter from Miss Susan Huntington and no letter for Miss Emily. Yesterday she burst into the kitchen after she heard the voice of the postboy and he was just after saying how bright the day was and the roadside flowers all in wild abandon – I think it was something that had been said to him for they did not sound like the postboy's usual words. And then of a sudden Miss Emily sweeps in like a brisk north wind and she asks the postboy, hopeful at first, if there is please a letter for her today, and she makes him check his bag again when he says there is not and she snaps at the boy and slams the kitchen door behind her when she leaves.

Now today she is a different woman and the kick of her legs has lifted her high into the air. She has taken up with sewing and that, I thought, was at least a distraction. And there is a ribbon in her hair today and I have not seen that before.

'Is someone expected this morning?' I ventured to ask.

She looked at me as though I was simple or one that might have lost her wits.

'What makes you say that, Margaret?'

It was the ribbon in her hair and the upswing in her mood, despite there was still no letter arrived; but I could not say that, not any of it.

'I don't know Miss Emily. Maybe there's a change in the air and I misread it is all.'

'I am not expecting anyone,' she said and bent her head again to her sewing.

Then later in the day and up is suddenly down. The change in the air was that it rained. A hard rain, hard like hammers and nails, which is something my mam used to say. And I had to close all the windows in the house and I noticed then that Miss Emily was not in the sewing room or even in her bedroom.

A movement in the garden caught my eye and it was Miss Emily in the rain. She was running here and there, her arms held in the air like a wanting embrace and she was calling and calling – not on her sister or her mother, not even on God, but Susan Huntington she was calling on, tossing the name of Susan in the air like men at the races tossing their hats when the horses have run well or won.

I could see the hem of her dress dragging in the mud and I knew I'd be sorry for that come Monday washday. But Miss Emily gave no heed to any such thing or to the coldness of the rain or to the water that must have been under her clothes and running in cold rivers down her back and over her breasts.

Like I said, love is a sort of madness.

I tried calling her name from the upstairs window but I don't think she heard.

Then she was knocking at all the downstairs windows and knocking at the doors and calling through the letterbox. By the time I got to the door she was gone again and I could only laugh at the comedy, knowing in my heart of hearts that laughter was sometimes the wrongfooting of me and that soon enough after there'd be tears.

When Miss Emily was eventually brought in from the garden the Mistress ordered me to heat water for a bath and could I prepare some hot tea with lemon that she wanted for her daughter and something light to eat, maybe a vanilla custard or a cake with cream and jam in it – by which she meant a Victoria sponge but she don't like to say the Queen's name in the house. And would I please be so good as to light the fire in the front room.

All of that carried out and completed to the Mistress' satisfaction and the rain slackened and soon had done with the day and stopped altogether. I visited the front room and asked if there was anything else that Miss Emily had need of – knowing that the one thing she most certainly had need of was beyond my power to provide. She waited till her mother had left the room and then from her clean dress pocket she produced a letter, all sealed and addressed and the same as a hundred letters she had passed to me before.

'It's for Miss Susan and must be in the post today or my heart will surely break.'

She din't actually say that about her heart surely breaking but in what she did say was the sense of what I have written or the feeling anyway.

'I will send a boy to the post and he will go all the way there for a piece of cake and no other payment, of that I am sure.'

There was a stillness in the house after that, like a held breath or like the quiet after a storm has passed. I held Miss Emily's sodden dress over a bucket of water and rinsed the worst of the mud from the hem. Then I hung it where the heat of the kitchen fire was gentlest and so would not stiffen the folds of the dress as it dried.

'Dear Susan, Susie, Sue, dearest and darling, please for to write soon and to put your letter in the post and a little extra paid so that it might be delivered all the faster. I was in the garden today but not to pick flowers or to listen to birdsong, but to drown. I swear it. The Heavens opened and I would have drowned in the rain had not my mother fetched me in. And now I do detect a cold is starting and I am quiet as dead cats and drawn into myself – a letter from you would, surely to goodness, lift my spirits. Even just a word to say each day you are thinking of me and love me and miss me. The loving is most important. Please Susan.'

I had taken to composing Miss Emily's letters for myself, imagining what I might find tucked into the folds of paper if, like before, she had pinned it unsealed into the pocket of her dress, what she might have written or what I might write for her if she had to ask. It was a fancy of mine, nothing more. There was not the poetry in me as there was in Miss Emily, but I knew what it was to be waiting overlong for love to be given back to me.

Then late in the day, so late I had thought to close up the house and make preparations for an early bed, there was a knock at the door, at the kitchen door and the postboy was there and he was whispering a breathless prayer for me to open to him.

'Please to tell Miss Emily that I am an ass and should deserve no less than a kick and will be sorry forever and to the last day of this life or any other life. I found a letter at the bottom of my postbag. It is addressed to her. It is the letter she has been expecting. I thought, even against the lateness of the hour, that I should bring it to you straight and so I am sorry for that too, for the disturbing of your evening.'

All his words came out in a rush, tripping over each other so I had to tell him to slow down and not to fret so. I assured him that Miss Emily would be too taken up with the joy of the letter for her to notice the lateness of the hour or indeed any other thing. And in that I was right, for she was daft as boxed frogs and leaping about the front room and just as mad as she had been when running about the rain-falling garden – an up-madness as compared with a down-madness, but it is madness all the same.

PS I should have said earlier but Miss Emily has acquired another companion. It is to be hoped that her spirits might be always lifted for now she has a dog of her own, a Newfoundland whose padded feet are so large and something to grow into, and his eyes do hang so that even when his tail wags he looks something sad. Miss Emily has given him the name Carlo after something she read in a book.

ADA ALICE PULLEN (iii)

I did not think he would but I asked him anyway. It was no nevermind to me if he did or didn't so when he said yes and he'd like to very much, well it quite wrong-footed me. I gave him the address of the theatre and the time of the performance and he came.

I did not see him in the audience and he did not wait to see me after the curtain had fallen and so at first I wasn't sure. But when I was next in his studio he showed me the notes he had made, notes on things he thought I should correct. There were words I said that made him shiver from the way I said them and things I did with my hands that distracted him from what I was saying and he said I had a way of standing that just was not natural.

Then he said he knew someone who could help and he'd arranged everything and I was not to be concerned over the cost for he had taken care of that also.

'She will work on your speech and nip and tuck those vowel

sounds that give you away. And something with the posture she can correct that too and what you do with your hands.'

He gave me a card on which was written a name and address and a date and a time. He had indeed arranged everything. I don't know, but I was sort of flattered by the length he'd gone to, not just going to the performance but looking with such a sharp eye at everything I said and did and then wanting to make me better.

After that, things began to look up. I don't doubt but Sir had a hand in that also. I was offered better parts and my name – the name of Dorothy Dene – began to appear in the column inches of newspapers and I was talked about and recognised in the streets or in the cafés.

'I still think that the theatre is no place for you,' he said. 'It is a place of scandal.'

'But I am applauded whenever I step out onto the stage and then again when I leave it. I am loved by the penny tickets and the shillings.'

He had finished the small picture of Crenaia. He'd described it as a jewel of a painting. He kept it on a second easel and waited only for the gentleman from Ireland to call and collect the painting.

'You will be loved by whoever looks on you,' he said gesturing to the painting.

'But no one will say as much to my face. Your painting will be in a gentleman's study and he will sigh when he looks up from his books and sees the nymph Crenaia half undressed and he will say her name soft as a prayer and he will make a noise somewhere inside, a moaning noise that is something between pleasure and pain. But he will not tell me, Dorothy Dene, that he loves me and wants more of me, encore Dorothy Dene, encore. Nor if it were in a gallery would there be anything for me in that for I have seen how men and women are in galleries. They are quiet as churchmen are when they are laying out hymn books for the early morning service and they stop and look up at the light falling blue and red and gold through the church window and they are moved almost to tears but they do not say even one word to that light. Even were I to loiter where a painting of me is hung, there would be no one to say bravo, bravo, and to throw flowers at my feet.'

He cleared his throat and busied himself with his brushes, wiping them with a bit of rag and setting the hairs straight. He did not look at me but had his gaze fixed on Crenaia and the words he spoke, so quietly I do not think they were meant for me or for anyone but for Sir himself, they stopped me in my rambling essay.

'But I love you,' he said.

It was not a declaration as such for it was whispered and had no celebration in it or joy. Nor was it anything I did not already know though it was the first time he had actually said it. Men are so easily known and Sir had let me know that he loved me in a hundred different ways. In how he brightened when I stepped into the studio, how he attended to my comfort even when I was naked and stiff from holding a pose for so long, how he pulled out the chair so I could sit with him to take tea and cake and he listened to my every word and waited until he was sure I was finished with what I was saying before speaking himself. And the small gifts – for after the pearl necklace, to be sure there were other such gifts: when I agreed to a project of his or when a painting was completed or sometimes for no other reason than it was a Friday. And how he looked at me, not just with the keenness of an artist's eye but something more tender too, and by that look alone I would have known that he loved me.

But now he had said it and there was no taking it back; now it was a creature in the room with us and not something hidden. Saying it changed things and though I could not quite say how I felt there was a difference in me and that altered how I was with him.

'When I see myself as you see me, in the paintings you make, I am come over with a feeling, a feeling that I want to conquer the whole world. I do not think I can do that from a gallery wall but maybe I can from the stage of a theatre for I think there are theatres across every country that is known.'

He set his brushes down and fussed over some other sketches he had made of me.

'I can help you in that regard. I know people.'

And so it was that Sir and I became joined together in this enterprise. Like a husband and wife we were. He bought dresses in my size and shoes and white gloves and he invited me into his house to dinner – surely the grandest house on Holland Park Road though it boasted only one modest bedroom and the bed in that room so small it only slept one person. He schooled me first in which fork to use and when and how to lift the glass to my lips and to sip at the wine and 'not to drink it like a roadmender drinks his tea'. And how to sit and what might be talked about at table. It was like rehearsing for a play. And one evening, there in Sir's splendid front room, I met an American theatre owner and he said he'd read my reviews – which I knew he had not – and he wanted to bring me to New York and to show me to the whole of the New World. He bowed like a nutcracker and I heard the crick in his knees. Sir took my arm and he said he was sure something could be arranged.

And I am certain that by the taking of my arm and the tender attentions he showed me, everyone in the room understood that Sir was in love. It was as plain as his beard and being friends with Sir they made much of me and brought me into the centre of their circle.

And maybe they understood that I loved Sir just the same for I absently caressed his hand when he held my arm and I looked for him when he was not near and caught his eye across the room and I must have smiled then for inside I was all butterflies and somersaults and my heart beat a little faster – as fast as ever it did when I was on stage and had lines and cues to remember.

'It will be your first American tour,' said the New York theatre owner and by that 'first' I was given to understand that it would be followed by a second and then a third and then many.

How could I not love the man who made all that possible, who took me to the highest point of the world and showed me what was to be conquered – now that I had conquered his heart?

And so I went to America and walked out onto a New York stage and the hush of the audience then was so loud it hurt my ears to hear it.

THE WEXFORD WHALE (iv)

Man's fancy does sometimes outstrip the practical. I worked with one Alfred Waterhouse on the designs for the new museum buildings, a 'cathedral to nature', extensions reaching wide to east and west of the original building. The drawings were detailed things of beauty and they got immediate approval from the board and costings were ordered and delivered and the government agreed to underwrite the whole project. Do not think that politicians lack for imagination, for it takes only a drawing and their spirits soar and they dig deep into their pockets and want to build dreams.

But the winged extensions to the Natural History Museum were not really the stuff of dreams. They were rather the stuff of cut-and-dressed stone, and metal and glass, wood and slate and terracotta. Even were the decoration to be scaled back, and maybe only one extension to start with, even then the cost would be enough to make a Queen on her throne blanche.

When the first sketches were drawn up – and oh but they

were beautiful and Alfred Waterhouse had lined the walls of the building with the skeletons of whales and sharks and dolphins and every other animal known to science and described down to the smallest claw or hair or scale in their scientific journals, and everywhere ornate columns reaching skywards and rounded arches and groin vaults and the panelled ceiling hand-painted and gilded and an endless variety such as reflects the world in its glory – well, the Empire was so rich it had money to throw away. But by the time the plans were more developed and the drawings, no less beautiful, but now only the arrangement of the walls and the windows and doors and weight bearing calculations and stresses and foundation depths and a hundred other confounding details, by the time these were completed and men in suits and stiff collared shirts and white gloves hiding the crimp and crumple of their hands had checked them and scribbled changes to be made to the designs in the margins and then new plans drawn and labelled, well, by then the world had moved on and the Empire was a little out of breath and a lot out of money. And the government, not lacking in imagination as I have said, had to cut its cloth according to its means.

The plans were scrapped, though Alfred Waterhouse insisted that they were only put on hold until better times greeted the Empire.

'The public might pay,' said one of the stuffy trustees at a meeting of the board.

And so began a campaign to raise the money privately, but these were straightened times for everyone and not enough money could be gathered up for even one stone-built wing. Instead, they threw together a makeshift pavilion they dubbed 'The Temporary', constructed of corrugated iron and big enough the Wexford Whale might find a home.

It is the way of these things, when cuts are made and a cheaper path is taken to the fulfilment of a dream, that in the end things don't quite measure up. Had they asked Albert Waterhouse to design their corrugated iron shed, I am certain he would have turned down the request in disgust, but if it were possible and he had been persuaded I am sure he would have come up with something fit for the purpose; but they ran with a cheaper architect and the maxim that you get only what you pay for was never more evident.

When the bones of the Wexford Blue Whale were measured and weighed it was found that 'The Temporary' was not to the right specifications to house such a giant and so the once 'Fish Royal' remained shut away in storage.

I have some of Albert Waterhouse's drawings still. The paper is yellow and brittle now and the drawings have lost some of their definition but they are still things of breath-taking beauty. A 'cathedral to nature' is what was asked for and a cathedral to nature is what Albert Waterhouse would have delivered. And the Wexford Whale would have had a fitting home.

I have heard it said that the bones sing. There was a woman who worked at the museum and she it was who told me. Only recently it was that I chanced upon this woman. She was crouched beside one of the boxes in the storage hall, her ear pressed to the wooden surface. Her eyes were closed as though she slept. Though her position did not exactly say sleep, I have seen workmen something the same, sitting upright with a cup of tea in their hands and their heads dipping into sleep and the cup slack and slacker in the hand so the tea spills onto the legs of the man and he does not immediately wake. That was how this woman looked, asleep and dreaming.

She must have heard my step and so she jerked back from the box as though stung or as though the box was suddenly hot as coals and burned her cheek. She was quite flustered and her face was in an instant pink and as though she had been discovered at some mischief or other.

She curtsied and made to go but I kept her back.

'What were you about just now?' I asked her.

'Begging your pardon sir, I was only listening,' she said.

'Listening?'

She then told a story of whale song and a man who was her husband till he went mad and he it was that had showed her where to put her ear to best hear it and I thought then that maybe she was a little mad also.

'I don't know, but it's a hopeful song,' she said.

'A hopeful song?'

And she showed me where to put my ear and instructed me how to hold my breath and to listen with every fibre of my being.

Like I said, maybe she was a little mad.

Afterwards, when I was seated at my desk looking over old drawings, I thought of what Albert Waterhouse had designed, a 'cathedral to nature', and I wondered if in that cathedral, had it been built to his specifications, a whale might have found a place to sing and if the sound of that whale singing would have filled all the rooms of the Natural History Museum even unto the panelled ceiling and spilled out through the open windows as much as the light spilled in.

Now there's a dream.

I have not dared tell anyone of my meeting with the whale-song-listening woman or of what I heard when I pressed my ear to the box as she told me to do and held my breath and listened with my heart as much as anything.

'A hopeful song' is how she described it. And the very air seemed to vibrate and it passed through me like a shiver. A hopeful song is right enough, I think.

EMILIE, EMILY, E (iv)

Miss Emily lives so much alone, by which I mean that she does not call on friends in the town or make daily visits to the stores or have visitors knocking at the door to take tea with her of an afternoon. It was just so before and is so still. 'She keeps to herself,' my mam would have said, but I never knew a lady so quiet with herself and so alone and yet not, I think, lonely – if she *is* lonely she does not betray her loneliness by pressing her face at window-glass looking out at the world, or by sighing when she thinks no one is listening, or by tears. And being so by herself I have perhaps invented a life for her that is more to do with my hopes than hers.

But oh may Saint Patrick and all the saints forgive my foolish heart; am I in error in believing that Miss Emily is in love with Miss Susan Huntington? Certain it is that she loves Miss Susan but that is not the same as being 'in love' with her. News has arrived today and such news that I think I *must* be in error and have built a whole world out of nothing but a few words written like poetry, and like poetry the meaning is as much in the person reading as in the words written.

A letter today, not for Miss Emily but for Miss Emily's mother – I ensured that the postboy made a thorough search of his bag in case there was also one for Miss Emily but there was none. As for the letter to my Mistress, it was from her son for I am well enough acquainted with Master Austin's hand.

I am not one to be listening at keyholes, but I confess that I did today and heard the Mistress announce the news to Miss Emily and her sister. And there was much jubilation in what the Mistress said and I do not doubt but the three ladies embraced and Miss Vinnie was dispatched with the news to find her father and Carlo would not let up with his barking, not though Miss Emily scolded him in that pretty way she does; and I was almost caught listening.

Back in the kitchen I was a little out of breath and my heart was racing and all my thoughts spun like feathered fairground sugar, which is to say cloudy.

And the news is that Master Austin is engaged to be married. That were news enough by itself but not so breath-taking news nor so heartbeat running news. Master Austin is engaged to Miss Susan Huntington. There and saying it out loud I was breathless again.

'I begin to hope for you', that is what Miss Emily had

once written to Miss Susan and maybe I was wrong to read it as I did. Maybe the hope that she had for Miss Susan was something to do with the love between Miss Emily's brother and her dear and darling friend.

Before even my thoughts had cleared and I could make sense of my silliness, the Mistress rushed into the kitchen and gave instructions for a cake to be baked and for port to be made ready in the front room and the best glasses brought down from the high shelf.

'It is a day of celebration,' she said.

I tried to look surprised and as though I did not already know.

'Austin is engaged.'

Then she rushed from the kitchen and back to the front room. Miss Vinnie and the Master and Miss Emily were all gathered when I brought in the tray with the crystal glasses and the bottle of port. I set it down on a low table and made to go, but the Mistress said I should fetch a fifth glass and take a part in the occasion.

I wanted to look at Miss Emily, to see how the news had affected her, but I thought that would have been too much like listening at keyholes with everyone looking on.

'It has been a time coming,' said the Master with his glass in the air. 'And now it is here I scarce do believe it. To Austin and to his bride to be.'

And we all lifted our glasses then and toasted the engagement of Master Austin. It was ten o'clock in the morning and we were drinking port. I do not know what people would think if they but knew.

As soon as I might, I made my excuses, set down my glass on the tray and left.

I was not sure how Miss Emily had taken the news. Was she a little quieter perhaps than she should have been at the announcement of her brother's engagement? Did her sister, Miss Vinnie, did she not obscure the quiet of Miss Emily with her gushing and the Mistress the same with the clapping of her hands?

The truth is – and there I go talking truth as if it is something that can ever be really known. Truth is not like fact, I think. The buttercup in the field is yellow, that is fact. Hold the yellow flower under a pretty girl's chin and if the yellow is reflected there then the girl likes butter; that is fancy. But truth I see now is something altogether different. Miss Emily loves Miss Susan Huntington, that is fact; that she is in love with Miss Susan is maybe only fancy, my fancy, and not as I had thought a truth.

Miss Emily kept to her room for the rest of the day. I was directed to take up a tray with a glass of milk and some cake in the middle of the afternoon.

'And maybe a winter apple.'

We kept the autumn harvest of apples wrapped in straw and in a box in the cupboard under the stairs. Miss Emily sometimes put her head in that cupboard and breathed in the sweetened breath of those sleeping apples. She said it must be how Heaven smelled all the time.

I fetched an apple and sliced the cake and poured the cold milk into a tall glass. Then I climbed the stairs to Miss Emily's room and knocked – a soft and dancing knock that I hoped might be thought merry.

There was no reply so I called to Miss Emily through the door and said that her mother had sent up a tray for her and that I was coming in.

She was, as I expected, sat at her desk, her head bent over her writing. Her fingers were blue from the ink. Carlo lay curled in a corner and he did not lift his head to mark my entry into the room. On the floor at Miss Emily's feet were the crumpled and discarded drafts of her writing. Maybe she was writing poetry, for I had seen rough drafts of some of her poems and there was much crossing out of what she had written and many alterations of the order of words, so many that sometimes it was difficult to read what she had penned. Maybe she was writing a letter, a hard letter, a letter to Miss Susan Huntington, and the words would not sit still on the page but stamped their feet and ran amok like a crazy woman, yelling and screaming 'no'.

All just fancy. Except that I could see Miss Emily had been crying, could see that she was crying still and her tears spilled onto the page in front of her and ruffled the paper, drowning the word she had written there and bleeding ink beyond the scritch and scratch of her nib.

'Your mother thought you might like a winter apple,' I said. I picked the apple up and held it under my nose and breathed in. 'I once worked for six weeks or seven picking apples in a great orchard in Ireland. I remember sitting in the back of a horse-drawn cart surrounded by baskets and baskets of apples and the smell of them made me dizzy, so much so that a boy of sixteen stole a kiss from me in the back of that cart and I had not the heart to scold him.'

I do not know why I said that to Miss Emily. Maybe I thought with the apple to tempt her away from her writing when it caused her so much distress.

'Miss Emily?' I said.

But she was not listening.

I set the apple down on the tray and stepped backwards out of the room – like fine ladies at court when they leave the presence of the Queen and they dare not turn their backs to Her Majesty for fear of giving offence.

And the truth is, with all those tears I still do not know if Miss Emily simply loves or is in love with Miss Susan Huntington. Not in my heart, which I have said already is sometimes foolish.

ADA ALICE PULLEN (iv)

Some days, when I read what was written in the newspapers about my performance, I did not care a fig or a tinker's tit for conquering the world. I tore those reviews into a hundred pieces and threw them out of the window, the scraps falling like snow on the street below. Sir said I was not to heed what some stuffy hack wrote in a rag that would be yesterday's news before it was even read. And he took me in his arms and he said my name over and over – not my real name but the name he had given me, the one I wanted the world to be calling and calling.

'I have another idea for a painting,' he said.

I did not know if he was talking to himself then or to me. He cleared his throat and began to tell the story of the painting. I think this was as much to take my mind from a thin-lipped and quite frankly mean theatre critic and what he had written about me.

'It is something from Boccaccio's *Decameron* and is the first tale told on day five. There is a lady sleeping in the woods, and such a beauty she is that it can only be you. I picture you draped and in sleep, your arms above your head as though you have given up everything to dreaming. The sun is going down, sinking below the line of the horizon. Indeed it is almost sunk. She is not alone this surpassing beauty. Children and handmaids lie curled into sleep at her feet and there's a young man a little way beyond her and he should be alert and on guard but he too has fallen into sleep. Only a dog is awake and maybe something has woken the dog for into the picture wanders a youth, uncouth and loutish, and he gazes on the beauty that lies sleeping and he is – well, he is quite affected by the beauty of this woman, it fills him up and in an instant he is changed and made soft and fine and good. It is a hopeful painting.'

I gave the story some thought before venturing to comment. That was something Sir had taught me: 'A considered word is worth a hundred tossed-in-the-air thoughtless words.'

'Are you the young man in the picture?' I said.

He laughed and he said he was not by any stretch of the imagination young, but I think he did see himself as that young man and like that man he was maybe changed by the seeing of me. Sir had not married before, had not even been interested, but now he held onto me as though I was his only hope in this world.

'It is something greater and will take months to complete,

so you must not go a wandering just when I most need you. It will be something for next summer's show at The Royal Academy and Miss Dorothy Dene will steal the show. Then they will write better words about you in their newspapers, you will see if they don't.'

He was trying to lift my spirits. I understood that and I did feel better listening to him and I put my hand to his cheek and held it there.

Sometimes I could feel the restraint in the man, like he was holding himself back. I am sure in that moment he wanted to kiss me, not gentle and not rough but something more than touching lips. I was certain that was what he wanted. I think I may have pressed myself against him then and made a small sound in the back of my throat, something soft and yearning.

'I think this calls for tea and cake,' he said and he broke from me and rang for a servant to attend.

Maybe I should have taken the lead. Maybe I should have kissed him and taken his hand and placed it on my breast. But what then? It was uncharted waters for I do not think there had ever been a woman in this man's life, by which I do not count a mother but think only of a lover.

'Does this sleeping woman have a name?'

'She is called Iphigenia which is also the name of the daughter of Agamemnon.'

'And the youth, does he have a name also?'

'He is Cymon.'

'And in the story by…'

'Boccaccio.'

'Does Cymon approach the sleeping woman and does he do more than stand and stare. Maybe he touches her hair or is so bold as to kiss her sleeping lips – for the young are ever bold. And maybe he lies down with her in her forest bed.'

'In the picture he only looks. Looking is enough.'

He pulled a chair out for me to take a seat at the small table. Then he showed me some of the rough sketches he had already made for the painting. He was filled up with light and love and excitement and all that was evident in his outlining of the picture and the colours he would use and the mood he would create and at the centre of it all Dorothy Dene asleep. Of course, I had not modelled for these sketches so he was drawing only on memory which is imperfect and the poorest cousin to observation.

'Months to complete, you said?'

'You will be mine and only mine for above six months,' he said.

'I will be yours forever,' I said in reply, by which I meant he would have me set down on his canvas and so captured forever. After, when I was replaying the day in my head, I thought perhaps he might have taken another meaning from what I had said.

Later and before we had quite finished our tea and cake, he was visited by a playwright of some distinction. He had arranged the meeting so that I might be better known to the gentleman. I'm not sure that I still had the appetite for acting, but this gentleman playwright was charm itself and so I let him kiss my hand and he gave me his card and Sir made me spin on my heels so the playwright might observe Iphigenia from all sides.

'She will conquer the world,' Sir said to the gentleman. 'You mark my words.'

As I made to leave, I heard Sir invite the playwright into the studio. The painting of me naked had already been collected and was by this time hanging on the wall of another gentleman's study, out of sight of his wife. But I knew that Sir still had the sketches and studies for the painting and that they would be brought out for the playwright to leer at. Sometimes I think there is no hope for men.

I should say that the playwright's name was George Bernard Shaw. I tucked his card inside a book I was reading and then some time after mislaid the book and so only have his name and not his address.

THE WEXFORD WHALE (v)

By the 1920s our understanding of whales had advanced beyond all measure and there was a public appetite for more. There was a need for the museum to improve and to modernise. It was reported on the letters pages of the London newspapers and then it leaked into the editorials and before long onto the pages proper with headlines to catch the eye.

'We should have a hall of whales with the Wexford whale at its heart,' said one of the trustees. 'Just imagine!'

I was a new member of the board and was just finding my footing and not yet finding my voice. I nodded and banged the table with my fist along with the other gentlemen, banging the table to show assent with what the speaker had said.

I'd read the story of the Wexford whale in a newspaper cutting that my father had pinned to the wall of his shed. I sometimes caught my father rereading the article over and over, saw him through the window so he did not know he was observed.

A hall of whales, now that would be something. Think of the visitor numbers and the merchandise and the revenue stream. But more than that, think of the contribution to science.

I had seen a whale once. I was aboard a fishing boat, with all the attendant discomfort of such a vessel. The man on the pier had promised a sighting of whales, though he also said the weather might be against us. He charged a shilling whether we saw a whale or no.

It was what might be called blowy and the sea seamed to boil underneath us and all about, and the fishing boat rose and fell on the swell so that standing on deck it was as though we danced or were drunk and not sure on our feet.

I saw the captain in the wheelhouse. He was speaking to the first mate and he shook his head and gestured to the sky by which I took it that he was commenting on the weather and perhaps on our chances of sighting a whale.

I went to lean over the side of the boat, feeling a heaving in my stomach. Then there it was, just breaching the surface, the barnacled back of a small Northern Bottlenose whale. I felt the breath from its blowhole on my face and that was enough to bring forth my breakfast, but it was no matter for I had seen the whale.

I turned and called to the others on the boat, but by the

time they had come along beside me the whale had gone under again. I think a sighting was reported a short while after but at a distance of maybe the length of two football pitches and in that tippy sea it was not certain that it was a whale and not just some swell in the water.

A hall of whales would surely be something and so I banged my hand on the table.

A letter was sent to the government and a commission set up to assess the situation. It did not take long to arrive at the only obvious conclusion: if Britain was to lead the world in all things, then we needed a hall of whales as an extension to the Natural History Nuseum. The money was allocated and the work began, by which I mean drawings had to be made and calculations of the load bearings carried out and the structural requirements listed. The wheels in such a vast bureaucratic machine turn very slowly indeed, but at least they were now turning.

I recall talking with a scientist who had studied whales and he'd written papers on their habits and behaviours. I asked him if it was true that whales in the deep of our oceans sang.

He said he had heard it himself. He had fashioned a brass trumpet into a crude listening device such as doctors sometimes hold to the swollen bellies of women carrying children and they do this to hear if there are heartbeats, the mother's and the unborn child's, only the scientist said his hearing trumpet was maybe twenty times the size. And he said he had lowered the bell of the trumpet into the great Atlantic ocean, near where he knew whales were gathering and then he heard it. And yes, it was like singing if singing was without the clip and cut of words and was instead something rolling and stretched, like a note held and then given rise and fall and dance.

'Others that have heard it say it is a sad song, a song that weeps or bleeds, but I think they characterise it on what they themselves feel for they have seen the whale-hunt and the water, enough to fill a great sea, running hot with the blood of the whales' slaughter and it is these scientists that have wept. For me the whale song is a love song and it is a song of some beauty and complexity. I should one day like to make a gramophone recording of it so that all the world might hear it. Then might the hunting of the whale stop.'

I may have nodded then, remembering how I felt when confronted with the Northern Bottlenose whale that day out on an old fishing boat and for which I had paid a shilling and would have paid ten times more for such an experience.

'And do they sing together, as in a chorus? And across species or just to their own? And are the songs the same each time they sing them or do they alter and are something extemporary like the new music in our dance halls?'

The scientist then scribbled in a black notebook that he kept in his inside jacket pocket. Only when he had finished writing and the book was secreted back in his pocket did he look up and offer an answer.

'The truth is, we do not know. I have only ever heard the singing of one song at a time and who knows how far it carries? Maybe from one sea to another, maybe across oceans. And do they reply to each other?' He shrugged and held his hands up empty. 'And how do they make such a sound? And what does it mean? We just do not know. We are only at the beginning of the story.'

In 1929 the government finally approved the plans that had been drawn up for the Hall of Whales. Funds were soon released and work began on the new building.

When I told my father, and he was something cut loose in his head by then and he some days did not know me for his son, but I told him anyway and when I did something in him brightened, like a room when an electric light is switched on. And I asked him then if he had ever seen a whale, a Northern Bottlenose perhaps, or a Fin whale or Minke whales. He nodded then, which is not to say that he had seen any such thing for he nodded at everything that was said to him, such was the advance of his dementia. But he sang to me then and he'd never done that before – not in words but in a deep humming song that came from somewhere inside him, rising up from somewhere deep, and his whole body trembled and there were tears on his cheek. Maybe he was singing whale songs.

When I thought about it afterwards, I was filled up with an unshakeable regret that I had not asked my father earlier about the newspaper cutting growing yellow and pinned to the wall in his shed, and why he read it over and over till he must surely have had the words to heart. I may have wept then – for the whales and their love songs and for my father and his.

EMILIE, EMILY, E (v)

Miss Emily was up before the lark today, but not before me.
The bread was still in the oven so she said she would just
take a cup of tea and that she would take it in the garden.
She had brightened again, almost seven months since the
announcement of Master Austin's engagement and nothing
seemed to have altered in the day-to-day working of the house.
And the postboy knew to quicken his step when there was a
letter for Miss Emily and she touched his hand and she said
he was sweet and she wrapped a piece of cake in waxed paper
and made a gift of it to him – only when there was a letter.
But then there had been letters enough and just as many as
ever there was before and some I have watched Miss Emily
open, for she is inclined to the garden when the sun is out,
and I have seen ribbons threaded into the page and pressed
dry flowers tucked in with the paper and tram tickets once
that Miss Susan had written on.

And there was suddenly talk of Miss Susan coming again to

visit Miss Emily and Miss Emily called her sister even though there was yet no date set for any wedding and Master Austin, when asked, only said 'by and by'.

When I took Miss Emily's tea out into the garden, she was sitting on the grass and reading again a letter that had come two days before. Carlo lay beside her on the rug she had set down on the grass. It was Miss Emily's habit to keep a letter by her at all times, in the pocket of her dress, pinned to the inside of the pocket so it never could be lost, or pinned and tucked into a book that she was reading, and when she had an idle ten minutes or more, then she was wont to unpin that letter and read it even though it could not have borne any news that she din't already know for she had by this time read it over twice or three times or more.

I could see in the margin of the letter Miss Emily was reading that Miss Susan had written 'love and larks ascending'. I supposed it was in reference to Master Austin and some fanciful comment on how Miss Susan's heart was lifted up by his love. But then when Miss Emily turned the page I saw that the letter closed with more than just 'affection' but with open hearts and kisses and love eternal and that was not anything of the sort that my sister wrote to me in her once-a-year letters. And so I dared to hope that I had not been wrong before and that Miss Emily was indeed in love.

I do not know why I should be so light in my step at this secret knowledge; indeed there could only be upset and hearts breaking in such a relationship, but you see, I know Miss Emily and I know the quiet she can be and the alone, which I now think *must* sometimes be lonely, and so for her to have someone near to her heart like Miss Susan, well, I think there is not a person walks this earth that does not deserve at least that. Nor is there a father or mother – surely – who would not wish as much for a fond daughter; even a father as stern as Mr Dickinson can sometimes be with his hat tipped always to God.

I cleared my throat, not for any other reason than to let Miss Emily know I was by with her tea. By the manner with which she pocketed that letter and the look of alarm against I might have seen something I should not have seen, I was confirmed that it was a love letter and that maybe Miss Susan had been a little indiscreet in her choice of words. At the same time, I thought I discerned some colour in Miss Emily's cheeks and that was to be thankful for.

I set the tea down beside her and a small plate on which I'd arranged a selection of biscuits, some shortbread fingers and petticoat tails, and something with cinnamon in and something with almonds.

Then I turned heel and made my way back to the kitchen.

From the small window there I could watch Miss Emily unobserved. She waited until she was sure I was gone and then returned to Miss Susan's letter.

'Don't let your tea go cold,' I found myself whispering.

When she had finished the letter she pinned it back inside her pocket. Then she looked about her, not for her tea or for the biscuits which I had arranged pretty on the plate. It was something else she looked for. I saw then that she picked a flower from out of the grass, a small blue flower. I should call it a forget-me-not if I were back in Ireland; I do not know if it is named the same here in Amherst. She kissed its petals and then carefully pressed it between the pages of her book.

'Drink your tea, Miss Emily, while it is still warm.'

Then she sighed, and so full of wind and sound was that sigh that I could hear it through the glass. And she got to her feet and walked to the end of the garden, followed at heel by Carlo, Miss Emily's head tilted to the sky and to the early morning sun.

Maybe it was a week or more later when I found Miss Emily's book, the one she had with her that day in the garden. She'd left it on the windowsill in the hall. I checked that I was quite alone and then riffled through the pages in search of that blue flower. I found the page where it had bled blue onto the paper but the flower was gone. This made me smile to myself, for I guessed that Miss Emily had tucked the dried blue flower into one of the several letters she had since that morning sent to Miss Susan.

I might have spared a thought for the young Master Austin then and the secret that he could not possibly know, and I should have been a little sorry for him, but he was out of sight and out of mind, whereas Miss Emily was very much present.

'Do you think, Margaret, we might have strawberries for when Miss Susan arrives? I do so love it when the berries, red as kisses or blood, are cut top to bottom and they look like small pretty hearts then.'

I made a note to buy strawberries.

'And do you think, Margaret, that there will be cherries and if there are please to get only cherries that come in pairs, their stalks joined together so that they are like sisters and can be shared like kisses?'

'It is a little early for cherries,' I told Miss Emily.

'And what say you, Margaret, to figs for I have heard the most outrageous things said about figs and I think I should like to be something outrageous with Miss Susan now we are to be sisters.'

No date had been set for Miss Susan and Master Austin to visit Amherst, only that they intended to come, so all this talk of strawberries and cherries and figs was just that, just talk.

Fancy. But to see Miss Emily so animated, well, to be sure I could do nothing less than join in her sweet games though she swore me to secrecy over the fruit she was playing with in her head and she put one finger across the kiss-pout of her lips and it was just as though she was thirteen all over again and not as she was, which was ten years added to that thirteen.

ADA ALICE PULLEN (v)

Maybe Sir had shown the painting-in-progress to his artist friends, or the sketches and studies he had made had been passed around. I can only guess at that for he never said this was the case. But one day, just as I left Sir's studio and was a little heavy in the body from holding the pose, I was stopped in the street by a Mr George Frederic Watts – that is how he introduced himself to me.

'Do I know you?' I said.

'You know my name at least for I have just given it to you.'

'Well, I'm not so sure that I have a mind to keep it.'

'You speak like a lady and you look like a lady and yet I know you are something other than that.'

He did not say less but he also did not say more. If anything he was older than Sir but there was a light in his blue eyes and a way he had of pursing his lips and smiling at the same time. Then I noticed the paint dried on the cuff of his sleeve and with that I knew him for a painter for Sir wore shirts that were just so spoiled.

'But in truth you are more beautiful in the flesh than in your picture,' he said, looking me up and down.

I did not think to ask which picture he had seen of me but was distracted by his cocksure confidence.

'I do not think a gentleman should be so bold,' I said, and I may have pouted and looked more cross than I really was.

'I have an idea for a picture,' he said.

I think I might have rolled my eyes at that. Sir had said I was not to do this, rolling of the eyes. He said it made me look as though I was losing my mind and should be housed in Bedlam and the key thrown away.

'I think we should know each other better before you start undressing me, Mr George Frederic Watts.'

He laughed then and in his laughter was the sound of words taking flight and I cannot quite explain it but I liked the sound.

He gave me his card then and he said I should call on him at my soonest convenience.

'I am already taken,' I said. 'I think you would have to ask Sir if I might be handed around like a gentleman's plaything and for an ungentlemanly price. I think Sir would have something to say about that.'

He waved one hand in the air as though he was chasing

off nuisance flies. 'You would be blindfold,' he said, 'In the painting, I mean. Sir need never know. No one would know. You yourself would not even know. Only I would know and don't ask me why but a part of me likes that.'

I must have scrutinised the address on the card then for he began giving me directions and said his wife would expect me and she'd escort me if an escort was needed. 'Everything above board and appropriately respectable for the newly educated Miss Dorothy Dene.'

He had my name – or a name at least – without I had given it to him. And he knew about the lessons that Sir had paid for.

'Some say that beauty is art's primary purpose,' he said, 'but I have something to communicate in the painting I wish to make of you, something important that will be like a light to the world and a guide to those in despair.'

'I am not in despair,' I told him. Perhaps he knew more about me, knew something of the modest apartment I lived in with my three sisters and that I shared a bed with one of them. And my father being absent for so long that I scarcely counted him a father, maybe he knew all this also, and so he thought I had every reason to be in despair. 'I am not in despair,' I said again.

Then he played his trump card and he knew the hand that he held was a winning hand. I don't know how he knew but

I could see that he did.

'I have heard that Miss Dorothy Dene has one wish and that is to conquer the whole wide world.'

I snatched for breath and held one hand over my mouth lest my heart escape.

'In my painting I am confident I can make your wish come true. I swear by all that is holy and good and fine. At least pay me a visit in my studio and see what I have to offer you.'

I must have faltered then for he put one hand on my arm and he said again that I should call and he said he would make it worth my while, 'For there is no price to be put on beauty and no price to be put on art.'

'I will call on you for a guinea,' I blurted out.

He pressed a pound note and a Queen's head silver shilling into my hand and he said he would expect me either tomorrow or the next day.

I later learned that he was a big name in the art world and he had money enough for a grand house and a young wife, at least a deal younger than Mr Watts was; and because he had no need of more money he had arranged to donate all his works on his death to the nation. This would secure his reputation and his place in history. And this benevolent old man wanted to paint me and gift me to the nation – it was not exactly the conquering of the world that I had imagined but I told myself I would be remembered beyond this life and that was something I had not given thought to before. I think only the old give this idea any consideration but now George Fredric Watts had put the thought in my head and it was a difficult thought to ignore.

My sister said I was a fool to think of going with every old man that stopped me in the street. She thought I was better than that now. 'You have, as they say, gone up in the world, sister. You wear fine dresses these days and 'ave three pairs of shoes and when you speak I swear I do hear a lady talkin. There's no need to be actin like a common street-walker,' she said. I pressed into her palm George Frederic Watts' silver shilling and that soon changed her tune.

'He's a famous artist, as famous as Sir, and he wants merely to paint my picture and is it not better to place two bets rather than just one, to take two bites of the cherry. This is my chance to conquer the world. I had hoped you might think better of me than a common whore. I am a actress and a artist's model and maybe a model for two artists, what is the difference when all is said and done, except my purse might weigh a little more when there are two artists paying.'

I did not tell my sister that a third artist, John Everett Millais, had also made advances and I had his card tucked into my purse. Men's hearts are so easily won.

THE WEXFORD WHALE (vi)

'Have ye a head for heights, lad?' he said, and I told him I had because Old Jim'd told me that was the answer they expected of me. There was a good deal of money to be made for a few months labourin and who knows but our names written down somewhere so we was part of history. I wasn't so bothered bout the history thing, that was just a old man talkin, but I sure could use the money.

It was for some butter-stone museum and we was to be puttin a whale back together, its bones at least, like it was a child's jigsaw only bigger, and then we was to set it flyin through the air like a bird. That's what Old Jim says to me anyway when I'm picked along of twenty other men. He was not to be believed. Old Jim told stories is all.

They gave us brown overalls so we all looked the same – different heights and shapes but somethin the same. And leather aprons we had to wear, like we was scullery maids or shoemakers.

To start with, we had to shift great wooden crates from one part of the museum to another. They was heavy enough I can tell you and it was as well there was wheeled trolleys to run em through the corridors cos I think shiftin three or four of em boxes with just men puttin they's backs into it, well that would have taken the best part of a fortnight and would've done me in for sure.

Then the boxes had to be broke open, but careful so nothin inside was damaged. There was a gentleman in a stiff collar and tie and a watch-chain hangin from his waistcoat pocket and he had his shirt-sleeves rolled up though he wasn't actually puttin his hands to any work; and he was overseein what we was doin. I think his name was Mr Gerald, or Gerrard.

We was in a great hall, like a church only bigger and the ceilin so far off. And sound just seemed to bounce like a ball off the walls, footsteps or callin or a hammer when it was dropped. And there was metal-twist cables droppin down from the ceilin and they held, suspended off the ground by only the height of a man, a great metal support. There was wooden trestles holdin everythin steady and takin some of the weight of that iron frame. Mr Gerald, or Gerrard, called it an 'armature' and he explained that it would hold the bones of the whale in place and maybe for a hundred years it would do that. He kept callin it the Wexford Whale but he never said why.

The bones was all numbered so it was known what would go where and everythin calculated and timed. Mr Gerald, or Gerrard, kept appearin and checkin his pocket watch to make sure things was runnin as they should. And slowly, piece by piece, we put all them whale bones back together. There was spaces between the backbones and we was shown how to pack those spaces with old newspaper and how to cover em over with plaster so the back looked like one straight unbroken line. We had to paint the plaster when it was dry so it was the same colour as the old bones.

The whole job took a little over three months.

I remember one day, Old Jim said it would be somethin to put our names to that whale and so we did – not where it could be seen but written onto the painted plaster and tucked out of sight.

'If it's goin to be flyin up there for a hundred years, by the time they find out we'll all be long gone and nothin they can do bout it then,' Old Jim said.

The head was the weirdest part of that great fish – I kept callin it a fish and Mr Gerald, or Gerrard, he leaned into me and said it wasn't no fish, it was a mammal. I reckoned if it swimmed in the sea then it was fish enough for me. The head was somethin ghostly. I'd seen the skull of a bird once, somethin lyin on a summer beach, and the whale skull looked somethin the same only the size of a house. I said all that to Old Jim.

'That's Darwin right there,' says Old Jim then and maybe what he said was clever and maybe it wasn't.

Then the cables, which was fixed to five points on the armature and ran all the way to iron fittins on the ceilin and then down to the floor again and fixed then to five points on the walls about the room, those cables had to be winched so that the whole blessed whale was lifted off the ground and free of the supportin wooden trestles. I thought we'd have it flyin by dinner time but we broke off early and just left the whale hangin. This was to check that they'd got everythin right and that the cables could take the weight of all em bones and the iron frame they was fixed to. All told it weighed more than a London bus and I could hear the crick and crack of the cables as everythin settled.

We cleaned up for the rest of the afternoon, sweepin the floor and clearin out the tools and the buckets of unused plaster and paint; and great tarpaulins that'd been laid underneath the whale so no paint was spilled on the floor, they had to be folded and taken back to the storage room.

We had more tea breaks that day than we knew what to do with and I felt like I was sweatin tea and I swear I could hear them seven or eight cups sloshin around in my belly when I walked.

'Be back tomorrow morning sharp,' said Mr Gerald, or Gerrard. He might have said 'early doors' which is somethin I had heard before but never really understood, 'cept maybe the 'early' I got. 'Tomorrow she flies,' he said, like he was announcin an act at the circus, and he went on about what a moment it would be and he said we was makin history and it would be in all the world's newspapers and he said we could be proud of what we had done. He said then how he was pleased that not anythin had gone wrong. Then he took out his pocket watch and tapped the glass in case we'd forgotten what he'd said about early doors.

The next mornin was where the head for heights came in. As the lightest of the team I was set to clamber over the skeleton as it was bein slowly raised into the air, makin sure everythin was balanced and even and one side was not lifted higher than another. At first it was no height at all, like lookin down from the upstairs window of a bus. But then I could feel the air between me and the floor, and more and more air, and Old Jim kept callin me 'monkey boy' and he kept askin if I was alright, like maybe I didn't look alright.

'Slowly, slowly,' said Mr Gerald, or Gerrard, and his arms was spread wide like a conductor in front of an orchestra and like it was him as was pullin all the strings just by the wave of his hands.

I was a little light-headed, I don't mind tellin you. When she was in place they lifted a great wooden ladder up into the air – high as Jacob's with all em angels ascendin and descendin – and I was to climb down; and Old Jim asked again if I was alright and if maybe I didn't want to take it a little slower and catch my breath and he stood underneath that ladder ready to catch me if I fell – that's what he said at least.

I don't know bout havin a place in history, not like some man called Ned Wickham who, accordin to the papers the next day, was the man what found the whale, found it just layin around on the shore at a place called Wexford in Ireland (now I understood why it was called the Wexford Whale). And maybe Mr Gerald Snr, or Gerrard Snr, the man who brought the whale bones to London, and his son, Mr Gerald, or Gerrard, well they might have a place in the history books, but I don't reckon anyone remembers the names of the workers what did the puttin together and the liftin, 'cept some of us put our names on the plaster links between the vertebrae and those names must still be there.

*

Some years later, when I had a boy of my own and he was nine or ten, I took him to see that flyin Wexford Whale and I pointed to where my name was exactly and I said how I'd once run from one end of that complete blue whale skeleton to the other, 'tip to tail' is what I said, and my boy laughed at that.

Only, I was wrong in what I said, for the skeleton was incomplete, missin a bone small enough it could fit in the close of my fist and nobody lookin up seemed to care, no one back when I was runnin the length of the whale's backbone and no one then when I was showin my boy where his dad's name was written into history. And the missin bone was the last in the whale's long back, the very tip of its tail, and missin that bone did not seem to lessen any the museum's boast that here was displayed the first complete blue whale skeleton, the first in all the wide world.

EMILIE, EMILY, E (vi)

Well now, but Miss Emily was some days lifted up and bright as angels, to be sure. But other days she was plunged into darkness. It was like she was a stringed instrument and when the air shifted it played upon those strings and if the wind was merry then the tune Miss Emily sang was sweet and dancing. But if the wind was gruff and heavy, then Miss Emily's brow was down and nothing was right with the world.

Is poetry like a bottle with a loose-fitting cork and it leaks, for I think my words are fancier today and do not sound like my own but like something the muse has gifted me. Poets talk of muses like they are something on high and looking down, and those muses put words into poets' mouths, and no doubt into their pens too. And that's what my talk of wind and stringed instruments feels like and I think maybe poetry has leaked out of me.

When Miss Susan Huntington came to visit Amherst, well that was a merry wind that blew and Miss Emily set time aside each day to call on Miss Susan and to deliver her a pretty posy from her garden and a pinned letter in the pocket of her dress – Miss Emily thinks I don't know about the pinned letters but I could see the glinting of the pin in the sunlight when she moved or could hear the small stiff crumple of paper or see the mis-shape of her pocket from holding them letters.

Then on her return from Miss Susan there was ever something pink in her cheeks, pink as pinches, and she moved a little lighter on her feet and Carlo's tail was lifted like a flag waving.

It seemed not to be a matter of any importance that Miss Susan was now two years engaged to Miss Emily's brother, Austin. Two years engaged and still no date set for any wedding. I did wonder why that was and if there was maybe some obstacle in the way and if maybe Miss Emily was that obstacle.

'There was a note came this morning with this book. Have you seen it anywhere, Margaret?'

Miss Susan was always sending books or bees in glass jars or pressed flowers in envelopes marked 'fragile' and I think those small gifts were just an excuse to write a letter to Miss Emily. Today she'd sent a book and, as it seems, a letter tucked into its pages and that letter now lost.

Everything stopped in the house so a search could be made

for Miss Emily's lost letter. That was a different wind blowing, even just for the ten minutes it took to discover where the letter was, and Miss Emily's brow was down and her tread was heavier then as though she was wearing her garden boots in the house.

I was the one that found the note from Miss Susan. Miss Emily had dropped it on the stairs. It was only folded and not pinned. I dared to look inside it. I know I should not have but I could not help it.

'I do not think that kisses always taste so sweet, dear and darling Emilie? I bit into a strawberry just now and it made me think of you, the sugar-sweet sap on my tongue and my lips pressed to the skin of that goblin fruit and its pink spittle juices running down my chin. Is it wrong to have you in my head, to think of 'two pigeons in one nest', and not to be thinking of Austin?'

There was poetry in there that did fly over my head as the blackbird does when it's frighted and it flaps its wings and cries alarm. No, I must speak plainer for I think sometimes poetry hides more than it reveals. I folded the note closed and exclaimed that I had found it and bent to put it back on the stairs so that when Miss Emily came in answer to my call she might see me bend to pick it up and so not think that I had read what Miss Susan had written.

I did not know what Miss Susan meant by 'goblin' fruit except that the book she had sent to Miss Emilie was called 'Goblin Market' by a poet with an Italian sounding name, the book published in London and sent across the sea to Miss Susan. Miss Emily kept the book hid from her father and so I thought there must be something in it that he wouldn't approve of.

The Mistress was to her bed by this time, by which I mean she was not well. I heard her some mornings and she was calling, not for me to bring her breakfast to her bed, but for Emily to bring it. And a dozen calls in a morning for Miss Emily to fetch her mother this or that or something. That was a burden for Miss Emily to bear, a burden she bore without complaint, one of a hundred burdens.

'I should like you to tell me how the day looks from the window of my room, Emily.'

'I wish for you to write a letter on my behalf, daughter.'

'Count for me the roses in bloom in the garden, there's a dear child.'

Then one day, and it was a day long after Miss Susan had returned to her home and still waited for a wedding day, and a more weighted wind blew into the house and Miss Emily received a letter with a black edge to the paper and it was news of a dear friend's death – not the dearest friend, which was

Miss Susan, but a friend that was dear enough.

Oh but could I lift some of the load that she carried then, but this was also something to be borne by Miss Emily, something to be borne alone for she could not bear the company of anyone and even Carlo was banished from her room and found a warm corner by the kitchen fire and curled into sullen sleep there to wait for better days. Maybe Miss Emily wrote of the death to Miss Susan; I think she must have, for letters were sent every day for the following week and one when I held it to my nose, breathed flowers.

Not even the garden had her attention at this time nor any of the children who leaned over the garden fence and asked after Miss Emily – not that Miss Emily spoke much with the children but they talked to her and they sang her songs some days and shared with Miss Emily their once-upon-a-star wishes; and Miss Emily listened, but not today or any of these days. Only her mother had her attention and only when she called.

'Sit and read to me,' the Mistress sometimes said and only then was the quiet of the house broken and Miss Emily reading was something musical and light.

I caught her as she was leaving the Mistress' room one late morning and I handed her a note of my own. I had not the fancy words of poetry or Miss Susan's way of expressing myself. I had written on a scrap bit of paper, the torn corner of yesterday's newspaper, a corner where there was no print and just the paper edge. I had written just one word – there was not space for more. I had written only 'hope'.

I do not know why that word above all others, why that word occurred to me and all the rest of language did not. I wanted that Miss Emily should have not just the word but the thing. Hope for what? Well, to be sure now, that was for Miss Emily to decide.

ADA ALICE PULLEN (vi)

Mornings I sat for Sir, or more correctly I lay down for him, my arms above my head and all of me stretched out on a mattress he had moved into the studio for the purpose and a dozen cushions besides. He had me wear a dress that he said was Grecian and something copied from a classical frieze – maybe the Elgin Marbles had women wearing such dresses, floating and like the movement of wind or air if such movement could be imagined in cloth.

Sir fussed over me as I feigned sleep, arranging the folds of the dress so that they were to his liking and so that they did not obscure the shape of my body beneath the dress but worked to reveal it. Sometimes I felt his palm lightly pressed to me, the warmth of me through the cloth rising up to meet the warm in his palm. It was innocent enough – not the innocence of a child perhaps but no intent beyond the briefest caress.

The silence in the studio was a little oppressive. He said I shouldn't speak, not even to rehearse my vowel sounds or even to breathe, though he sometimes cleared his throat or when he lifted his brush to paint some upper corner of the painting and he groaned, if by groaning can be understood that he breathed heavy and made a small sound somewhere inside and it was as though he was lifting more than a paintbrush above his head and something nearer to the weight of a table or a bed.

After the morning had drifted away and he'd painted only a leaf on the tree or the glint in Iphigenia's dog's eye, we took tea and cake together and it was then in these moments that we could talk.

'I need the afternoon to myself,' I said to him.

'Are you shopping for shoes then, or is there a play to audition for or does your sister need your help with some sewing?'

I did not think there was anything to be gained and much to be lost by telling him the truth so I kept it from him. I was in the afternoons sitting for Mr George Frederic Watts and his important painting.

Mr Watts was always pleased to see me. And in truth I was pleased to see him. He had more life in him, I think, and he asked after how I was – 'How is Miss Dorothy Dene today?' – and he asked if it was warm enough in the studio before we began work. His wife brought in a tray with a jug of water on it and two glasses and lemon cut into rounds and small cats' paw cakes that she said were French and they had a French girl's name that sounded like Mary-Janes and which tasted a little of roses.

There was a separate room where I could change – for Mr Watts wanted me dressed in something Grecian also, though the fabric of this dress was thinner and you could see me through the cloth. Mr Watts used the word 'diaphanous' – I later learned what that word meant and wondered if Mr Watts didn't think it described myself as much as the fabric. I sat on a hill of cushions and he made me cross one leg under the other. I held in my left hand a musical instrument that he said was a lyre – he had copied the design from something in the British Museum or he had someone make it to a drawing he had made of that lyre, only this one had a single string and I was to be in the act of plucking that string and me leaning over, all my body crooked and angled as though I was straining to hear the music of that one plucked string. And I was blindfolded as he had said I would be.

'You do not have to wear the blindfold all the time, just when I am painting your face particularly. And it is a difficult pose to hold so we will stop often so you can rest.'

'Will that not slow the painting down, Mr Watts?'

'I can afford to linger. And every hour will be another guinea in your purse.'

He made a sketch in oils first. It had a lot of blue in it and was a rough mapping out of the composition. He showed me the sketch when it was done or when he'd had enough of it.

'I want a little more of the face. I have seen the blind and how intently they listen, not just with their heads cocked and their ears pricked, but with their whole bodies it seems.'

He made me walk about the studio for a whole afternoon wearing that diaphanous dress and the blindfold and he crept up on me and I was to listen for him. It was a child's game but he said it would teach me what it was to be blind and to listen and that would help with the picture.

He showed me the oil sketch and it was something beautiful and unfinished. The hill of cushions was altered so that it was as though I sat on a great ball, a ball such as I had once seen an elephant balance on in a circus ring. I remember sitting alone in the cheapest seats – maybe I had stole into the tent unseen or I had found a farthing in the street and that had afforded me entry – and the thick air smelled of spun sugar that is sometimes a little burned, and so many people all sitting pressed together in a small hot space, and a man dressed in a black frock coat kept shouting at the audience – not crossly but shouting all the same. And music was playing all brassy and blown. And I remember there was an elephant that looked grey and heavy and sullen and at the crack of a whip it slowly climbed up onto a great wooden ball and it stood on the ball, balanced and still, as though it was something painted and not living. And here in the painting by George Frederic Watts I was like that elephant, sitting instead of standing, but atop a great ball the same.

'It will be as though you are Atlas's sister, if ever he had a sister and she was blind and played on the lyre. It is the world you are sitting on.'

'He had only brothers,' I said.

This caught Mr Watts by surprise. He held the pose as though I was now painting him, his eyes wide and his mouth slack and open.

'It was in a play I read for once. Atlas had brothers but no sisters. I think he had daughters. I think the nymph Calypso was a daughter of Atlas.'

He paid me at the end of each session. He totted up the hours and exchanged them for guineas and made a record of the payments in a book that he kept in a desk drawer in his studio. Mrs Watts always came in near the end of the afternoon and it was her entrance that seemed to be a cue for Mr Watts to begin to clean his brushes and to lay an oiled cloth over his paints and to stand back from his work.

He asked his wife then what she thought. She slipped her arm in his, locked together, and she looked more intently on what Mr Watts had painted. Time seemed to stand still in these moments and there was a heightened air of expectation in the room and maybe Mr Watts did not breathe and his hopeful heart beat a little slower and a little quieter too.

Then Mrs Watts declared it was better than all the words he had used to describe it to her, better than the scribbled sketch he had done without me in it.

'It is just a sketch also for I am working through the colours and the mood.'

'She really is most beautiful,' said Mrs Watts.

Mr Watts kissed his wife's cheek and patted her hand on his arm and breathed.

And like that it was as though I was not there at all, or was there as a fly on the wall eavesdropping in on a couple that after so many years were still fond and gentle with each other, though I later learned that the shared years had not yet been so many and maybe the newness of their love was explanation enough for how they were with each other.

'Have you told her yet?' said Mrs Watts.

'Not yet,' he said.

THE WEXFORD WHALE (vii)

It's Mr Gerrard, Charles Gerrard. Sometimes Mr Gerrard Junior on account of his father, Edward, being known as Mr Gerrard Senior. No 'Gerald' anywhere. He was, if I remember correctly, a very careful man and gentle and inclined to be loquacious at dinner, indeed even when he was by himself!

I got the story from him, which is to say straight from the horse's mouth. He had consumed a glass or two of wine with his dinner and so his tongue was even more loose than it was wont to be. He took me into his study and we sat beside the fire each with a glass of port.

'Can you keep a secret?' he said.

I never knew him as a gossip and so I knew this was something else altogether. Maybe he was to be presented to the Queen for his service at The Natural History Museum or he had come into a bequest or had won a pocketful of money at the races. I nodded and by that I hoped he understood that I could indeed keep a secret, even an after-dinner and two-glasses-of-wine secret.

'You will be familiar with my work on the Wexford Whale,' he said.

There was a newspaper cutting showing the whale skeleton and Mr Charles Gerrard standing beneath it with his hands tucked into his trouser pockets – there's a picture of the great engineer Isambard Kingdom Brunel posed just the same in front of the launching chains of the SS *Great Eastern*, except that Mr Charles Gerrard is without any hat and without a cigar. The newspaper cutting was mounted and framed and behind glass on the mantelpiece above the fire where we sat.

'I am familiar,' I said.

He leaned a little forward and I mirrored him and like that we must have looked like two bookends.

'It was a busy time when we were putting her together. 252 bones, if I recall correctly. And a team of workmen who didn't know a fin from a fiddlestick. I was overseeing every small detail and when it was almost all come together it was an exciting time. You know my father brought the whale over from Ireland and the bones had languished in a dozen storage crates for almost forty-two years and here at last I was completing my father's work.'

'He would have been so proud.'

'Hold on there,' said Charles Gerrard. 'Let's not put the

cart running ahead of the horses.'

He took a sip from his glass, set the glass down on a low table and leaned in again.

'On the second last day, the whale was fully mounted on its iron armature and we lifted it off the ground, not so high that if the cables didn't hold it would end in disaster, and we left it like that overnight. It was a way to check the stresses and strains on the cables. The whale bones together with the iron frame weighed above ten tons.

'After the workmen had clocked off for the day and the evening was tending towards dark, I took a moment to myself in the great whale hall, a moment with the Wexford Whale and me and maybe the ghost of my father. I swear the whale shifted a little and the cables creaked under the weight and then settled again. And there was a dull moaning sound, as though the bones had been struck and like a tuning fork they vibrated and gave out a strange music. I fancied I heard the sea there in that great hall, fancied that the Wexford Whale was at home at last and the cold waters of the Irish Sea covered over me.

'I must have fainted then, which I suppose was more to do with how tired I was for I hadn't been sleeping well and the work had occupied my thoughts to the exclusion of all else for near on four months. I woke, lying in the dark of the whale hall and she was above me, the Wexford Whale, and I was under her and we were somehow joined. Strangely, I thought of my mother then.'

Mr Charles Gerrard paused in his story and I thought that was it, that was the secret that he had thought to share with me. After dinner stories can be like that, both something and nothing.

He revisited his glass of port and maybe I made some comment on the story as it had been told. 'That's quite a tale,' or, 'Was your mother a big woman then,' or maybe I started in on a story of my own, 'I fainted once…' But Mr Charles Gerrard held one hand up to stop me proceeding.

'There's a tail end to my story to be told first,' he said and chuckled to himself as though there was a hidden joke in the words he spoke. He replaced the drained port glass on the low table.

'The next day they lifted the whale up to the ceiling where she still is to this day. I heard one of the workmen say she was flying like a great beaked bird. I stood back a little in awe of what we had achieved. A photographer from the press was invited in and he took a picture of the workmen with me in the centre of the picture. Then he wanted one with just me and the whale. It is that picture you see there,' he said, pointing to the framed newspaper cutting on the mantelpiece.

'See me standing like Brunel, with my hands stuffed into my pockets. And do you think, looking a little closer, there is a smile at the corner of my mouth?'

'Yes, perhaps the beginnings of a smile,' I said.

'And that's because I have in that moment, just as the photographer snapped his picture, discovered something that is embarrassing and awful and funny all at once.'

He paused then, as any good storyteller might. He nodded to me for he was just about to drop the secret on me, the something I was not to tell anyone not even my own wife.

'In my pocket,' he said, 'I discovered the caudal vertebrae of the Wexford Whale, the final tail bone, what might be called the whale's coccyx. Small enough it could fit into the palm of my hand and my fingers close over it and you'd never know.'

I must have snatched for breath or held a hand over my mouth, holding back laughter or horror.

'The first complete blue whale skeleton on display for the whole world to see and it was not in the end complete!'

He laughed a little uncertainly and I think he slapped his thigh and sat back in his chair.

'The hall had been cleared by then and the scaffolding trestles dismantled and the cables fixed. It seemed such a small thing in my pocket that I thought it might never be noticed nor missed. And indeed that has been the case.'

I was lost for words and sat with my hand still covering my mouth.

'I have it still,' he said, and he nodded and looked just like a child who has carried out some mischief and not been yet caught.

He got to his feet, walked over to an old Victorian kneehole desk. He withdrew a key from his waistcoat pocket, unlocked one of the drawers and removed something from inside. He brought it back to show me. Wrapped up in a soft off-white cloth, like an unwashed handkerchief, was something that had shape and misshape. He held it out for my inspection.

'Bone number 252, the last bone in the Wexford Blue Whale's tail.'

Perhaps there was something in the way I looked at him, something that did not need to be put into words for it was as obvious to him as it was to me. He nodded, took the bone from me and in silence he wrapped it again in the off-white soft cloth.

'It must be returned, of course, but I am not sure how.'

We kicked that football around over several meetings until we reached a conclusion. It was decided that I would return it for him and that this would not happen until after the death of Mr Charles Gerrard and it should be done quietly and discreetly so saving him and his family any embarrassment.

At the last meeting a lawyer was brought in to witness our signatures put to a document that stated everything I should do and I was given a copy of the key that fitted the lock of the drawer in his desk where the bone was kept.

I do not know what it was in my person that prompted Mr Gerrard to entrust me with this task. I never asked. He poured two glasses of port, gave me one and then we drank without another word being spoken. That was the last I saw of him. Mr Gerrard passed away not more than three months after.

EMILIE, EMILY, E (vii)

Master Austin and Miss Susan are married and a three year engagement is not so unusual as to raise eyebrows. Not Master and Miss now but something joined. And the Mistress got up from her bed to join the celebrations and that was something to talk about in itself and that gave rest to Miss Emily for she was not called upon to fetch this or that, or to read to the Mistress to while away the time for above an hour.

All attention was then on Master Austin and Miss Susan – the new Mr and Mrs Dickinson. And no one looking to Miss Emily and how she held her hand to her heart – checking it was still beating – and her breath a little quick and snatched as though it was something she knew not how to do anymore. I saw all that and the way she looked at Mrs Susan which is the same that Carlo looks up at Miss Emily wanting only to be petted and spoken to.

But the news did not stop at a wedding for the new wife and her husband were to live in Amherst and not just in

Amherst but next door in The Evergreens house.

Then, like a stage trick worked by directing the attention of the audience elsewhere, Miss Emily took Mrs Susan Dickinson in an embrace and I saw her slip into the bride's dress pocket a folded tatter of paper, something torn from the bottom of a letter perhaps. Quick as quick, Miss Emily's fingers nimble as mice. So now my attention was all on Mrs Susan Dickinson, waiting for her to discover the love note from Miss Emily in her pocket and her face all candles when she did for she would not know how the marvellous trick had been worked but be delighted that it had.

Then I saw Mrs Susan Dickinson take a small lace and embroidered handkerchief from her pocket – the same pocket – and she did not see the note from Miss Emily come out with the kerchief and it fell to the carpet and floated under the armchair. No one saw it but me.

When everyone was moved out into the garden I crept like a thief into the front room and retrieved Miss Emily's note to Mrs Susan Dickinson. It was not a letter as I had expected, but was a poem instead. A single verse, all dashed and dashes so that reading it was a breathless rush.

'Hope' is the thing with feathers –

Miss Emily had taken my 'hope' and made more of it than the one word I had gifted her – was it a year ago now?

'Hope' is the thing with feathers –
That perches in the soul –

Feathered and perching made me think it must be a bird,
but then I am not really schooled enough in poetry.

And sings the tune without the words –
And never stops – at all –

Did she mean that she had hope and that her hope would
never wither? I thought maybe she did and I thought I must
know what that hope was and it was of no matter that Miss
Susan Dickinson was married now for hope takes wing and
flies above that – which was, I think, another of the muse's
lines and not really how I would say it at all.

I folded the paper closed and looked to find a way that I
might magick the poem back into Mrs Susan Dickinson's dress
pocket, though my fingers were not so quick nor so nimble
as Miss Emily's.

*

And one year lies on top of another and another and we were
all looking to see if Mrs Susan Dickinson lost the shape of
a girl and found the shape of a woman which is sometimes
something swollen and ripe. But all the looking was in vain.

And Miss Emily was at the Evergreens every day and

every day she had a song in her mouth and always a secret in her pocket. I thought the drawer of her desk must be full to bursting with all the poems she had written and the letters she had received and the small dress-pocket notes from Mrs Susan Dickinson. I could not think there was so much to write about in the day-to-day of Amherst, but they seemed to chatter like birds, if letter-writing might be thought of as chattering.

And Mr Austin, he was sometimes with his mother in the front room here and they talked in stony whispers and – as the saying goes – I do not think all was rosy in Mr Austin's garden. But then that is to suppose and to guess and not ever to know, for no one really knows what goes on behind closed doors not even when things are written in letters or books.

A man delivered groceries today, to the house. He called at the kitchen door and he said he had come instead of the usual boy but he did not say why, if the usual boy was sick or had broken a leg or suffered some other mishap that prevented him being the usual boy. And I offered the man tea and a slice of cake and sat with him at the kitchen table and like that we passed the time of day. When he got up to go, he said, 'Well now, but this was nice,' by which I took him to mean the cake, 'cept he leaned into me then and kissed me – not on the cheek which would have been affront enough, but his lips to mine. And that might be said to have occurred behind closed doors for the back door and the kitchen door were both closed, and no one knows 'cept me and the delivery man.

*

Miss Emily had to see a doctor about her eyes and the doctor was in Boston so she was away for a few days and staying with cousins in Massachusetts. I never knowed the house be so quiet before. Carlo loped from room to room checking for Miss Emily behind the curtains and under the beds and when he laid hisself down beside the kitchen stove he did so with such a heavy drop that I knew he was well and truly sunk and I think maybe he had lost all hope that Miss Emily could ever be found again.

And the Mistress called on me these few days, to bring her tea in her bed and to draw the curtains against the brightness of the day or to open them again to let the light in. I didn't read to her for she says she does not like my reading, says it stops and starts like a jackdaw stammering and loses all sense in the holes that is made in the words and sentences. I do not tell her all the faults in my reading is a result of my schooling, nor that I was once thought the best reader in my class. Miss Emily went to a finer school than ever existed back home in Tipperary and her reading is like birdsong – and I do not mean jackdaw song but something closer to lark. I understand the Mistress preferring that Emily read to her.

And Mrs Susan Dickinson dropped by the kitchen when Emily had been gone for two days and she asked when it was that Miss Emily was expected to return – though Mrs Susan knew full well – and she asked if there had been a letter to say how Miss Emily was and if she was missing us in Massachusetts. Mrs Susan Dickinson left a bouquet of flowers, which is more than a posy and was enough to fill two vases, and she asked if I might arrange them in Miss Emily's room for when she was home again. There were roses in the flowers she had brought and they would give the room a sweeter air.

And the usual delivery boy was absent again and the delivery man had taken the usual boy's place. Indeed, this had happened so many times now that I thought that 'usual' no longer belonged to the boy but rather was owned by the delivery man. He took tea with me and cake – I had come to expect him and so there was always cake for when he did deliver. And after the tea and cake he kissed me, not as the first time but a whole jugful of kisses and so I did think he loved me and I think maybe I loved him back, for I looked for him coming each and every day and when I heard him whistling and could not yet see him then I was emptied out and moths or butterflies filled my stomach and I held my breath with my hopeful fingers crossed, asking God or his angels to please let it be the usual delivery man and not the boy. And when it was not, then I stamped my foot at the boy and closed windows hard and shut doors with a slam – which caused the Mistress to ask if that was Miss Emily returned.

ADA ALICE PULLEN (vii)

I should have known that I couldn't keep everything secret and hidden. The blindfold I wore in Mr Watts' studio was not something to hide behind but was as when a child plays peek-a-boo and it covers its eyes and thinks it cannot be seen and then it lowers its hands and cries 'peek-a-boo' and laughs at its own conjuring skills which we can play along with but is not really conjuring at all.

'I hear you are sitting for Mr George Frederic Watts?'

Sir just dropped it in as casual as that, every word measured and balanced and even so I could not tell if he was cross or hurt or did not care at all.

'Some afternoons,' I said, not wanting to say too much in case Sir had heard more than that I was just sitting for Mr Watts.

'Is it a painting?'

I nodded and must have looked a little like that cat that's done wrong and it pretends that it does not know what it has done.

'Is it a large painting? Does he intend to show it at the academy? What is the subject?'

'Mr Watts never asks about what you are doing or anything at all about you save to hope you are well.'

Sir was quiet then and shut up like a cupboard that is locked.

I went behind the screen and changed into the Elgin-marbles dress, then I lay down on the mattress and cushions and waited for him to adjust the folds and furrows of cloth to his liking. This time he was careful not to touch me through the dress and neither did he linger as he was apt to do. Then he hid for the morning behind the canvas on his easel and did not say a word but cleared his throat often and sometimes coughed.

Even when we stopped for tea and cake, Sir had few words and so I was glad at last to take my leave of him and if Sir was looking from his studio window I am sure he must have seen the spring in my step and my hair flying behind me as I hurried to Mr Watts and his young wife. My father once said time spent in misery was long and time spent happy was quick. It was before he left our lives that he said that – at least my mother reported him as saying such, though it was also something she trotted out when the day had been harder than most; I thought in substance what was said was right. The time spent with Sir that morning was slow and the time with Mr

Watts that afternoon was quick.

Mr Watts' painting was taking shape. I think he sometimes worked on it when I was not there so that when I was posed before him all his attention was on me, the folds of the dress, the tilt of my head and the way I cradled the lyre and plucked at its single string.

There was a delicacy to the brushwork, not the sharpness and detail of Sir's painting, but a softness and a tenderness. When we stopped for tea and so I could unfold myself and rub the stiffness from my neck, I stood for above a half hour just looking at myself in Mr Watts' painting. There was an unutterable sadness in the work too, such that I was pulled into it and my heart went out to the poor blindfold girl and I swear I could hear the music that she played on her one-string lyre and it was the music of yearning and love lost and hearts breaking, and still she played on.

I wondered about my mother and father then. I wondered if they'd ever nursed hopes for the future, a shared hope perhaps. That things could be better for them and between them. They must have been happy once. In love too. They must have been. And somewhere, I think, they lost hope. It is not so easy to see the stars when you are down in the gutter. I swore an oath then, silent and sore, that I would never lose hope – hope that things could be better in this world for me and for my sisters. Time stood still then or it leapt like a green frog from out of the cup of my hands and back into the green river and was gone.

'What do you think?' said Mr Watts.

I was so lost in the looking that I had forgotten he was there in the studio with me.

I tried to speak, to put into words what I thought, even to have thoughts, but all I had was weeping and tears.

'Oh Miss Dorothy Dene,' he said and he took me in his arms and he held me as tight as not ever letting go and he stroked his fingers through my hair and said, 'There, there.' I felt like a small child woken from sleep and wanting the comfort of a parent and finding it that afternoon in Mr George Frederic Watts.

When Mrs Watts came into the studio at the end of the session she found us still held in each other's arms and Mr Watts must have looked at his wife and said with his eyes what was what. Mrs Watts looked at the painting and then she put her arms about us both and she wept too.

How could I say any of that to Sir? How could I put into words what the painting was? And then say about being held and not let go for the longest time. And Mrs Watts joining us. Even telling my sister it felt somehow wrong to be putting into words what had happened.

Mr Watts had said on that day that we'd met in the street – not by chance as it happens but by design, for Mr Watts had been waiting for me – he'd said then that he wanted to help me conquer the world. I never for one moment thought that he meant anything in that. For that reason I had asked for a guinea just to meet him. Now, seeing the painting, and it was not yet finished, but already I was conquered and so I thought the world would be too.

'What is the subject?' Sir had asked me that morning.

'I don't know really. Maybe in the painting I am a nymph or a nereid and she plays on a lyre and it is as though the whole thing is seen through green water or glass, or tears.'

That was about as near as I could get to saying what it was.

Sir only nodded and he turned his attention to the mixing of paint and the selecting of brushes. I went to change again behind the screen.

Then, from out of the silence of Sir's studio, when I could not see his face and he could not see mine, spoken with only love and the boldness that comes from being hidden, Sir said, 'You will make a beautiful nymph or nereid, the most beautiful.'

I may have wept again in that moment and, though Sir did not move to hold me or to give me comfort in any other way, still I took some comfort from what he'd said.

THE WEXFORD WHALE (viii)

A letter came into the museum in the late '70s or early '80s. It was on headed paper and there was something legal in its construction and the phrases it was couched in. I have only a vague recollection of the letter. I was a young clerk then and everything was new to me and so I thought letters of this sort were common. It said something about the Wexford Whale and a bone that was missing from the tail. I passed the letter on to 'upstairs' and gave it not another thought, except that I sometimes visited the hall of whales and looked up at the great blue whale and looked for where a missing bone might go.

It was not unusual for things handed upstairs never to be heard of again. Upstairs was upstairs and downstairs was down.

Then sometime in 1987 a second letter came in. I took a copy of that letter and that is how I know the year. It must surely have come from the same person as before, though without the first letter to compare it to I cannot swear to it. It also said that our blue whale was not complete but was missing a bone. The bone had a name in this letter which I do not recall it having in the first. It was the caudal vertebrae from the very end of the blue whale's spine. The letter was addressed specifically to one of the upstairs team and was accompanied by a small padded box in which was a plaster cast of the missing bone, which was only missing from our whale and not in itself missing for it was in the possession of this letter writer. I made a note that this was the second letter that the museum had received regarding the matter of a missing bone from the Wexford Whale and again passed the whole matter upstairs.

I am led to believe that the first letter was somehow lost but not before a carefully worded reply was made and which considered the matter dropped. I do not have a copy of this reply so am not sure of what was said. But this second received letter, after being read by 'upstairs', was consigned to the archive and no reply drafted or sent. Perhaps the boxed plaster cast of the missing bone was filed away along with it.

It was in 2015 that a third letter arrived at the museum, marked for the attention of the Director. There were at this time plans to move the whale to a new location; it had been hanging in the whale hall for eighty-one years and it was thought the skeleton might benefit from some renovation.

A letter was sent in reply to this third letter, drafted by upstairs and typed by one of us downstairs. It made some small excuse for the error, something about the numbering of the bones when the whale had been boxed up in Ireland where it had been found sometime in the 1890s, and how imperfectly the numbering had been done and how this had resulted in the oversight and the missing bone.

The return of the bone would be most welcome. I remember that was one line from the letter and an invitation was extended for the bearer of the bone to visit the whale hall where the Wexford Whale was being readied for the renovation work prior to its relocation.

The missing whale-bone arrived well-wrapped and in a box carried in the hands of a man who introduced himself to me but whose name I immediately forgot. The bone was examined and judged to be just as described, the missing final bone in the long line of the female blue whale's spine, and it was recorded and set aside until it could be put together with the rest of the blue whale skeleton.

When the hall of whales was cleared so that the cables could be released and the whale skeleton and its iron armature lowered to the floor, I was charged with taking some notes on the condition of the bones. It was clear that the skeleton wanted more than just cleaning, even though the layers of dust had given the whale a thick furry skin. Some of the bones had cracked and split and if it was to hang in its new location for a further 81 years then a job had to be done to stabilise the whole skeleton. It was a bigger job than anyone had imagined.

The team had to be expanded and a more detailed programme of inspection and testing embarked upon and a calendar of deadlines drawn up and a final date arrived at for the unveiling of the blue whale in its new home.

It was also decided that the whale should have a new name, one that fitted the generation it was being prepared for.

I noticed that on some of the plaster links between the vertebrae and underneath the thick pelt of dust was written the names of what I assumed had been some of the workmen who had been active in the construction of the whale skeleton back in the 1930s. Some names were also written on the jaw bone of the whale including a 'Mr C Gerrard'. A note was made of all of these and the names recorded in the museum's archive.

I brought my eight-year-old son in to see what the restoration in action looked like. It was one of those 'bring your child to work' days. I lifted him up so he could read some of the names written on the plaster links.

'Someone called 'Old Jim',' he said.

Then, when the museum was closed at the end of that day and everyone had gone home, we visited the whale skeleton again and had it quite to ourselves.

'It was reported somewhere that whalebones sing – in the

dark of the museum when everything is quiet and still,' I whispered.

'I heard whalesong once,' my son replied. 'Mum played me a recording of it. She said whales lie on the bottom of the ocean and sing in the hope that somewhere on the other side of the world there's another whale listening.'

We stood in expectant silence then, listening, looking up at the blue whale skeleton.

My son said then that he thought the whale looked sad. And he said maybe that was because it missed its family. It was a strange thing to say but also perfectly natural. It would also prove to be wonderfully prophetic.

EMILIE, EMILY, E (viii)

I heard that Mister Austin and Mrs Susan Dickinson have another child to partner the son that had earlier been born in 1861. I must confess that I do not know the name of this child for I am no longer a part of the family and no longer at work in their kitchen. I was told it was a year after I left that Mrs Susan and Mr Austin were so blessed and delivered of a girl. I sent a card but have yet to receive any reply.

It was the delivery man that took me away from Miss Emily and Miss Vinnie and the Mistress, not that he stole me away for I went willingly and even gladly, though I was sorry to leave Miss Emily behind and I could see that she would take my place in the kitchen until such time as a replacement was taken on.

The delivery man should have a name and so I tell you he is called Martin and he kept calling and calling till he finally called me away and we are married now and it was done properly and before God in a church. We are not so far from

Amherst but then not so near neither. And business is good enough I have a Sunday dress alongside my weekday dresses and my Sunday dress is white as clouds and the hat I wear with it is yellow as buttercups. And there is a child on the way and I did not expect that – a child on the way, I should perhaps have said that before anything else for it is my first thought each new morning and my last thought each night before sleep overtakes me – and every step I tread is the heavier for the carrying of that child. Martin says he will have to widen the doors before too long – which is only a joke Martin makes and is not to be thought a truth about my new size – though I have had to let out the seams on all my dresses. And we have a dog that sleeps at the foot of the bed and she is called Posy which is like 'poesy' and is maybe something Miss Emily would have liked.

I think of Miss Emily near every day and wonder if that little bird she called 'Hope' still sings in her soul. And I wonder about Mrs Susan and if she is now more in love with Mister Austin and a little less with Miss Emily. And if she is, then I worry for Miss Emily for I do not hear that there is a man in her world that she might one day be engaged to and then one day wedded to.

I wrote to her about a year after I had left. I thought a letter after so long a time might be allowed.

Dear Miss Emily

I hope I might be permitted to write to you like this and only on occasion, though I do not write near so well as you or Mrs Susan. Please to begin by telling your mother, the Mistress, that I wish her well and hope she is not too much to her bed but taking a walk about the garden some days and smelling the flowers and talking to the birds. And to the Master please pass on my best wishes and thank him for the extra monies he sent as settlement of my wages. And to Mister Austin and Mrs Susan, I hope they are well and taking joy in their new girl. I sent them a card but they must be taken up with parenting so much that they have not had time yet to pen a reply.

And now to the letter proper, for it is to you, Miss Emily, that I address this letter. I am happy with Mr Martin and I dare to say he is happy with me. But there is a part of me that is still there with you in Amherst and I think of you often and wonder how you are and what you are about now that I am not there to see it all with my own eyes.

I can, of course picture how it is. I can see you early doors, but not bread oven early, sitting on the grass just beyond the kitchen door, the door ajar if the day is warm or the window open just a crack so I can hear you talking and talking to Carlo, telling him your heart's secrets, which if I heard any I never would tell, and speaking to him of the flowers growing in your garden, such a fine garden, and the birds letting their songs fall down on you from on high, larks I think you once told me they were.

But then you are the lady of the kitchen now and so I think you must be up bread oven early after all and so I see you tired and your hair pinned up from your pretty face and already falling loose in wisps across your cheek.

And washday Mondays, I can see you pink and flushed and leaning on the dollie-stick, the sleeves of your dress rolled up above the elbows and your breath coming short and quick as though you have wrestled a bear or a lion.

I hope you have time in your day for poems and letters, Miss Emily, but if not then a simple one word note to say you have received this is all that is needed, though I'd rather have a letter filled with hope dressed in feathers and singing in the soul.

I have pressed into the pages of a book – something I saw you do so often – a small pink flower whose name I do not have but which I saw and thought of you and thought it might make you smile to see it – you must have time for smiles Miss Emily. Please find the pressed flower enclosed herewith.

Martin has his own shop here and I am a help to him in the business and we pay a local boy to be our delivery boy and the postboy is called Stephen and I told him I was writing to a dear lady called Miss Emily and he said that 'Emily' was his most favourite name in all the world and he has four Emilys on his

postal route and he especially looks for Emily letters to deliver. He
has said he will come back at the end of the day and pick up this
Emily letter and see it on its way and all that for no extra charge.

And so I must close and be waiting at the front door of the
shop for Stephen the postboy. I hope it may be allowed that I close
this letter with love.

From Margaret O'Brien that was once your kitchen maid and
washerwoman and cook and front room servant, and postwoman
when the postboy did not call. Margaret O'Brien who is a wife
and will one day soon be a mother, which is the news I so wanted
to share with you, Miss Emily, and have kept for the last word.

As soon as I put the letter into Stephen the postboy's hands,
or at least as soon as he had turned the corner at the end of
the street and could no longer be called back, I regretted one
thing in the letter I'd sent. I regretted that I'd said what I'd said
about wishing for a letter filled with 'hope dressed in feathers
and singing in the soul'. I thought from that Miss Emily might
know that I had read the scrap of poem she had placed into
the pocket of Mrs Susan's wedding dress and which had fallen
out with a handkerchief and I had picked it up and got it back
into Mrs Susan's dress pocket – but not before reading it.

When no letter came in reply by the end of a week I
thought it must be that; I thought Miss Emily must take me

for a keyhole snoop and be glad to be shot of me. I was cross with myself then and cross at the world.

I think I must have been out of sorts with every customer one day and maybe I shut the shop door a little too heavily after one of them for Mr Martin said he thought he would need new hinges for the door before too long if I was to close the door so hard again.

ADA ALICE PULLEN (viii)

I arrived ahead of our arranged time on that last afternoon – the last for this painting at least. It was Mrs Watts who answered the door. She was all smiles and she said she was pleased to see me and that Mr Watts would be with me shortly. She led me into the studio and I think she was a little excited to be just me and her in that church-like space and with the light spilling in like water.

'He will want to show you himself, but it is almost finished,' she said, indicating the painting on the easel which had been covered over with a stained cloth. 'Indeed, I think he will not add anything to it today and maybe not tomorrow or any other day. I think he just wants your company again this afternoon. He has grown fond of sitting with you when the work is done.'

I was concerned that if there was no work to be done that day that I might not get paid for the hours. That is to say, the thought of not getting paid crossed my mind but then just as soon left me again.

'Has he told you yet?' she said.

'Told me what?'

I expected Mr Watts had another painting in mind already. That's what Sir did when a painting was almost completed in his studio, he sketched out his next idea and placed me into it.

'Has he told you the title for the painting?'

I shook my head. I'd assumed it was some mythological subject which it had not taken me long to realise was the fashion in painting. The Grecian dress and the lyre gave me also to think that. I was not educated in the way of the classics and so I was not so very interested, but I could see what pleasure it brought men like Mr Watts when I pretended to be so.

Mrs Watts put one finger across the smallest pout of her lips and she pulled back the cloth on the painting. I caught my breath again and felt a tugging near my heart, something like love or loss. It was clear that Mr Watts had worked on it some more in my absence. The painting looked finished and I could not see any part of it that needed for adjustment.

'It is as he said it would be,' I said, but I was speaking more to myself then and so my words were hushed. 'It is me and yet the blindfold hides me. And I am sitting on top of the world.' It did look like the world in the painting and I was playing the lyre, plucking a song from the one string, a song which the whole world was listening to.

'It is called 'Hope',' Mrs Watts said, her lips to my ear as though it was a secret she shared then with me.

I felt as light as air in that moment and as though my feet lifted off the ground. I thought I must be in a faint, but I did not swoon or fall. Mrs Watts kissed my cheek then and tenderly.

I am no art critic and have only known painting these past few years so nothing I say can carry any weight, but all the elements of Mr Watts' work said to me it was perfect. He had added a single point of light at the very top of the canvas and it was I think a star in the firmament, and I swear I have seen that star and wished on it maybe a hundred times when I was young. My sisters had wished on it too. All we had was wishes then, and we snatched them out of the air and kept them in our tight closed fists and hidden in our dress pockets, which is a thing small girls do – wishing for fortunes or fine dresses or love. But in that moment, the moment I discerned the star in the painting, I thought maybe this was everything I had ever wished for as a child.

Mrs Watts had been right to say there was no more work to be done to the painting. We were served tea and rosewater-scented cat's paw cakes and we talked of when the painting might go on show and in which gallery. Mr Watts said he had taken the liberty of already showing it to some friends and one had offered to purchase it for a price that spoke to the man's desperate need to have it and to the depth of his pockets; but Mr Watts had promised the painting to the nation along with all the other major works in his possession, and so he said that he planned to paint a copy for this other gentleman. He said he would use the original painting for this purpose and so there was no need for me to sit again and he gave me an extra two guineas just to copy my likeness so.

'But, Miss Dorothy Dene, conqueror of worlds, do not think we are finished,' he said.

'Because you have an idea for another picture?' I said, and I may have been hopeful in my asking that.

The next morning, when I turned up as usual at Sir's studio, he looked me square in the face and I thought he might forget himself and kiss me – though, as he had not kissed me since that very first day, in my heart I probably knew he would not. He pulled me after him and into his studio. Then, when we were quite alone and unobserved, he said, 'It is finished.' There was a question in his saying that and so I knew he did not refer to his own painting, which had another two months in it at least. I understood that Sir was asking after Mr Watts' painting that was indeed finished.

'Has someone run ahead of me and told you?'

He shook his head. 'It is in your face,' he said.

I took off my coat and made to go behind the screen to undress and dress again in a heavy Grecian tunic that had more cloth than must ever have been practical.

'Well?' said Sir.

I must have shook a little, my hands at least and so I held them behind my back. 'I think you will have to see for yourself,' I said.

'Has he painted you beautiful?' he said.

I considered my words then, as Sir had taught me to do, as a lady might do.

I thought Sir only wanted for me to say yes and I might have given him only that, except that I was still in a reverie over the painting and had not yet spoken to anyone on the subject, not since it was finished. Not even to my sister who had only this morning remarked that I'd been a little restless in my sleep and she'd wondered if I was not well or troubled or had lost something dear.

'I know it is me in the painting,' I said at last, 'and you will also know it is me, but I am blindfold and crimped and crumpled as though I might fit in a box or an envelope. The eyes, as you know, are windows to the soul and so I do not think anyone else seeing the picture will know it is me. But the painting... well, it is quite beautiful and so full of heart and feeling and...'

There was a quiet in the room then and I could see Sir was hanging on my every word and particularly hung on the last word that was briefly held back.

I placed one hand lightly on Sir's chest. 'Hope,' I said, 'It is a painting full of hope.'

Maybe my hand pressed too heavy on his heart or the air in the room was suddenly thinner or Sir had fallen under some spell or other. I leaned into him and whispered for him to just breathe.

THE WEXFORD WHALE (ix)

Our teacher, right, he was nice and all that, and interesting, but he was daft too. He taught us science and a lot more besides. He had this space on the wall beside his desk at the front of the class and he just about covered it, floor to ceiling, with pictures of things he took an interest in. There was black and white photographs of old men, like Darwin with his dinner-napkin beard and his beady eyes. And there was Marie Curie working in her lab doing stuff on radioactivity, and Gregor Mendel who looked like a vicar and he was the father of genetics with his green and yellow peas, though no one knew that until long after he died. But not just men and women of science, he had a colour photograph of the moonwalk, and that was Neil Armstrong in 1969, and a picture of the structure of DNA, and a photograph of a whale suspended in the air and he said it was the blue whale in the Natural History Museum in London and his dad had taken him to see it when he was a boy – it was hard to think of our teacher as having a dad or being a boy.

All sorts he had on that wall and each picture was a story and on a good day you could get Mr Boland – that was our science teacher's name – to talk about one of these pictures and he could fill a whole lesson with talking and we'd not have to write a single thing down so it was easy just listening – and it wasn't the science we'd be tested on so we didn't even have to listen, except the way Mr Boland told stories, well, he kept you listening.

He'd get carried away, see, with the story, and he used his hands and his arms so you could *see* the story he was telling, and his whole body too, and his face so lit up and his voice, well I said once it was like his voice danced or jumped or kicked. Kev who sat beside me, he punched my arm and called me soft when I said that about Mr Boland's voice dancing and jumping and kicking.

'You're as daft as he is,' Kev said.

I remember this one day and a girl at the back of the class asked Mr Boland if he had seen something on the tele the night before – we sometimes arranged it so the prettiest girl in the class would ask a simple-seeming question and that might kickoff one of Mr Boland's wonderful stories or a daft story, either way always an interesting story. This girl, the prettiest, her name was Moira and she asked if he had seen the programme about the whale on the TV, the same whale that he had a picture of on his wall and that his father had taken him to see when he was eleven.

Mr Boland stepped from behind his desk and we knew then we'd hooked him, like some great fish, and we sat back to watch him kicking and gasping for breath and a whole story spilling out of him. To be fair, he always tried to link the story to science in some way and looking back it was all learning.

He pointed to the picture on the wall and he said they'd taken that whale down from the ceiling where it had flown for more than eighty years and they'd cleaned the dust from the whale skeleton, eighty years of dust and they collected all that dust in a bag to be tested and examined. Dust don't hardly weigh nothing at all, but they got more than three pounds of dust from that whale! And dust attracts moisture and that can damage the bones so they had to examine the whale skeleton too, every inch of it.

And then they had to take the whole jigsaw puzzle of the whale apart.

Kev said that when his mum finished a jigsaw she just tipped the whole lot into a box, tipping it in all anyhow so it was a minute to take apart what had taken days to put into a completed picture that matched the one on the lid of the box.

Mr Boland set Kev right. He said that whale bones was not like jigsaw pieces exactly and they could break and splinter and the people in the museum didn't want to just put the pieces in a box and that box placed on a shelf to be forgotten about. They had plans to put it all back together and to hang the whale in a different place – someplace called the Hintze Hall, a space that was like the inside of a church with pillars and arches and a descending and ascending great staircase. It's funny how much of Mr Boland's story I remember – the small details and all recalled without really trying to and against how little of the science we were tested on has stayed with me.

Science, Mr Boland said, had come a long way in a hundred years and he waved a hand at the pictures on his wall. And I fancy his attention lingered on one photograph in particular, a photograph of Mr Alan Turing in his Hut 8 standing beside a computer the size of a room. And Mr Boland said a team of computer scientists took pictures of every bone from the whale and made a 3-D model of the whale in a computer-generated image of the new space and they computer-printed the whole whale skeleton and they built a scaled-down Hintze Hall and they arranged the computer-printed bones in the hall so they could see any problems there might be in the way it was hung. Some job that was, he said, and it was hard to disagree.

It seems the whale that Mr Boland had seen when he was a boy, well, it was hung all wrong and the museum wanted to put all that right and they wanted to make the display of the whale fit for a modern audience and so it had to be more natural and at the same time something dynamic. There was this one man, Percy Stannick or Stammer, or something like that, and he was given just one job and that was to come up with a new design for the whale skeleton, a new pose. He was thorough though. He went out to see how blue whales are in the water, sailed out on a great rubber boat, almost no sound in that boat so it wouldn't disturb the whales. And he quietly watched them surface, again and again, breaking the water and gasping for breath. Then when the whale was filled up with air, it spread wide its pectoral flippers, like a bird opening its wings, and it arched its back and dipped its nose and dived, the tail following the arc of the whale's body and at the last the tail lifted out of the water in a delicate kick. The whales were diving for krill, Mr Boland said, and krill are like small shrimp and that's food enough for blue whales which he said are as long as two buses standing bumper to bumper.

They fitted monitors and cameras to those watched blue whales and they recorded everything so that this time the whale in its new pose would be perfect. Then they went back to their 3-D models and they constructed a carbon fibre armature for the whale bones to hang on, and this had to be almost invisible and they hung the model whale skeleton on strings and they had it diving for krill with its jaws open wide and its pectoral flippers like it was flying and the curl of its whole spine and the tail kicking.

Then the real bones had to be weighed and the stresses and strains calculated and the building had to be tested just the same so the whale skeleton wouldn't pull the whole hall down. And the team of experts just kept growing and people from all over the world came, bringing with them a small piece of the whole jigsaw. That's what Mr Boland said anyway.

But the best bit of Mr Boland's story was what he kept till the last – which was often the way when he was telling us something. They found a box in the storage area of the museum, see, and it contained the blue whale's baleen. Mr Boland explained what that was. Blue whales don't have teeth, at least not beyond a certain stage in their development. They have teeth when they're born and then they don't have them and instead they have baleen and this is like teeth and like nails, made the same and made out of keratin, and the whale uses the baleen to filter out the water when it swallows a huge mouthful of krill. People once used this baleen, which is strong and bendy, to make women's corsets or collar stiffeners for men's shirts. Well, here was a whole box of the blue whale's baleen and so they did some tests on that and they found out all sorts of amazing stuff about the whale. They were able to map its last seven years of life – the whale was maybe fifteen years old when it died – and to show where the whale moved in those seven years, the pattern of feeding in the north and then when the north was too cold the whale holidayed in the warmer waters of the south, off the coast of Spain.

But then they found evidence of something else, something that made the story somehow bigger and better. They found evidence that the whale had given birth to a calf, maybe a year before it died. Some of the girls went 'aaaaw' when Mr Boland said that and I sort of understood why because suddenly the story of the whale had feeling in it. Blue whale calfs stay with their mothers for maybe ten months, feeding on a milk that's one hundred times more nutritious than a human mother's milk. And at the end of ten months the calf is independent and mother and baby go their separate ways. It was after this, when the mother whale must have been tired from the months of feeding its calf, that she became stranded on a sandbank off the coast of Wexford, stranded and without the strength left to free herself. There was something sad about the death of that blue whale but also something beautiful.

Mr Boland was so alive when he was telling us this last bit about the calf and it was almost like he could not believe it. More than a hundred years after the death of the whale and they were able to tell stuff about its last seven years, right down to the giving birth of a calf that might, even now, be swimming about in today's waters.

'And that's why science matters,' Mr Boland said, which is what he said at the end of every story he told and just as the school bell was ringing for the end of the lesson.

And I think Mr Boland is maybe right in what he says about science and I think maybe when I leave school I want to be a scientist too. I told him that one day and he just nodded and smiled and he patted me on the back as though we were related somehow.

EMILIE, EMILY, E (ix)

Dear Margaret

You must forgive me for not replying to your letter before now. I might say that I have been busy in the kitchen – a whole year or more of washday Mondays weighing heavy on my time and Mother in her bed for all of that year – she still asks me to read to her each day and to fetch and carry for her – she now has a brass bell beside her bed and the ringing of the bell is sometimes a summons unto duty, which some days does feel a little like slavery. All of that might be excuse enough for the lateness of my reply, but the truth is that I set your letter aside as something I should get to in due course – the letter was then lost, slipped between the covers of a book in which I had pressed a pink flower – then the book returned to its place on a whole shelf of books and that book not taken up again until today – today your letter is rediscovered.

You say in your letter how I sometimes pressed a pink flower between the pages of a book – this you had seen me do, not just pink but blue and yellow and red flowers also. And so I think you will recognise the truth of my pressing your letter into a book also and losing it in just that way. It is something I do often – then am always pleasantly surprised to make a discovery – as I was to find again your letter.

For your letter, dear Margaret, I offer an overdue thank you. I am so uplifted that Margaret is happy – even if selfishly I might wish her back again with me so that I am not so much in the kitchen or so early. Do not share this with Martin but tell him I wish him well and I wish him prosperity – in all things.

You ask after Mrs Susan and I should say she is changed, which is I suppose a natural consequence, in part at least, of being a mother now and weighed down with all the worries that being a mother entails. I do not think Mister Austin is always kind and perhaps that has also changed Mrs Susan. I try to find time in my every day to see my darling sister, but she is so taken up with dear Ned (which is my affectionate name for her son) and also with Mattie, her daughter – and dear Mrs Susan always so tired, that I do not think she picks flowers as she used to – nor do I think she writes so much as before.

As for Mother – as I have said she is to her bed and does not see the garden except as I am called on to describe the view from her window. She is, I fear, something shrunk since you were last here – like a small child – she must be coaxed to eat and she does not smile or say thank you or in any other way express pleasure in her day. I am careful to select something light to read to her each evening, but I do not think she hears the words – hears only the music of my voice which is to her like the humming of a bee and nothing more to her than that.

Father is, I believe, well – though his work takes him from us sometimes – even when he is with us I can see that his thoughts are often elsewhere and so it is as though he is not here at all. But I think he is well and he gives himself to his work willingly.

But come, I do not want this letter to be filled up with grey clouds, Margaret, for that is not how I would have you remember us.

I was in the garden today – the bread was set for its second rise and the oven was coming to temperature and mother still slept, so I had time to take a walk about the garden. I danced then – can you picture me dancing? There was birdsong threaded on the air – larks and linnets I am sure. And the sound of bees was all about me. Indeed, one bee was briefly caught in the folds of my dress which I gently shook – it tumbled onto the grass and did not for a moment know which way was up and which way down; then it rose up before me and it was as though it inspected me, head to toe, and finding no threat it flew round me and off into the sky. And I danced then, and would have sung except I was no match for larks and linnets so instead kept my song inside.

I do recall, Margaret, that you once handed me a slip of paper on which you had written just the one word. I think I was in low spirits at the time and this one word was intended to be a key to unlock the sun. You should know I have that one word still and I look at it sometimes and the sun does indeed shine when I do. 'Hope' is the word you wrote – I have written a poem about hope that I think, from something you said in your letter, you might have read a verse of; maybe you overheard me reciting the poem to Carlo when we were sitting together in the garden. No matter, but you should know I have written down the thing I most hope for and I should like to share this confidence with someone.

My dear and darling sister – by which I mean Mrs Susan – she would be the one to share it with normally but she is, as I have said, taken up with making a family, and so, if I may I should like to share it with you. I read somewhere that young girls do some days write the names of the young men they love, on scraps of paper or cloth, and then they throw these into the fire – just above the flames so that the singed paper or cloth is lifted into the chimney – carried to the heavens where stars make wishes come true. My writing this hope to share with you may be something the same.

But I cannot put it down in a letter, one which you may wish to keep and to read over again and again, or tuck into a book to be found in some other time. Instead, I write it on a torn piece of paper which I hereby enclose and I ask that you read it and then destroy the paper – maybe toss it into the fire, just above the flames so it is sent up into the stars along with the names of young men who are loved and wished for. Please, Margaret, in this you must be true and do as I ask of you.

But hark I hear the ringing of a brass bell and must answer the call. I close in haste therefore – sending you my fondest best wishes.

E

And how my heart yearned to be back with Miss Emily when I read that letter, to be of some assistance to her and to her mother, so that all their lives might be a little easier. I kept the scrap of paper that was enclosed with Miss Emily's letter, kept it pinned into the pocket of my dress, just for one day and then another. And when I was by myself, I took it out and read over what she had written. Then after two days, my conscience pricked, I did as she had asked that I do: I dropped that piece of paper into the fire. It did indeed fly up the chimney as Miss Emily had hoped it would and maybe up to the stars – I do think that it did.

Now, when I recall that secret hope, and I do not have the paper by me, I find I cannot remember with any clarity the fine words that Miss Emily had written and have only the rough gist of what she wrote. She hoped, against her father's wishes and maybe her mother's also, that she might be a published poet one day and her name printed on the cover of a book and her name known beyond the horizon of Amherst.

She had by this time – I think I am right in this – one or two poems printed in the pages of a newspaper or periodical, but what she truly hoped for one day was for a whole book.

ADA ALICE PULLEN (ix)

Mr Watts had written the address for the Grosvenor Gallery on a piece of card, the dates and times for the exhibition. It was a gallery in Bond Street. Sir said that it was a small gallery for work that might not be shown in better places like the Royal Academy's Summer Exhibition. I do not think there was any judgement in what Sir said.

I didn't tell anyone when I would attend the gallery, preferring to go alone and not to be made a fuss of. I wanted to see for myself how the painting was received. My eyes alighted on 'Hope' as soon as I entered the gallery. It had a whole wall to itself and was situated in the best light and just where it most caught the eye.

'The prime spot,' is how Mr Watts later described it.

There was something of a crowd gathered around the painting and so I did not go towards it direct but feigned an interest in some of the paintings on the other walls.

Then, by small and slow steps, I came to where the

attention was most focussed, to Mr Watt's painting of 'Hope'. I positioned myself not so I could see the painting but so I could take account of the faces of the people looking at the painting. One small girl, maybe nine or ten, dressed in a dark blue coat with silver buttons and a red scarf that was carelessly thrown over her shoulder and it hung down her back like a fallen flag, she was quite overcome and she had one hand over her mouth and her eyes were wide with wonder. And her mother – or it might have been her aunt or her nanny – was the same picture of stricken dumb. Others were so caught up that they wanted to say something, and I heard a gentleman begin the same sentence six times and not ever finish it and he said, 'I do think it is a dream and it touches my heart and it …' and I so wanted him to complete what he was saying but it was as though he lost his words and so he began again in the hope of finding them and then lost them again.

'Is it 'Hope', but I do not think she ever was blindfold before and yet now I think about her I do not see why not?'

'And is it a lyre she plays upon? But it only has one string so I think it is a rather hopeful musician that she is.'

'Do you see the star, mama? Star light, star bright, first star I see tonight; I wish I may, I wish I might, have the wish I wish tonight. It is the wishing star, mama. It is the first star, oh I do hope that it is.'

'But isn't it sad, do you not think it perfectly sad? And hope against all odds is just like that, is it not?'

Of course, there were those who did not like the painting, and they shook their heads and looked cross and turned away, but for the most part the reception was positive. I saw one young gentleman wipe away a tear and he thought he did so in a way that was not marked by anyone else in the room, but I marked it. I found my way to beside him when he was further into the gallery and I stood shoulder to shoulder with him in front of another painting and I slipped my hand in his, just to see what it would be like. He did not snatch back his hand or in any other way show surprise, but softly squeezed my fingers in his. And like that we stood in silence a while, and I do not think our attention was on the painting in front of us or on each other but still lingered on the picture of 'Hope'.

I told Mr Watts about holding this stranger's hand in the Grosvenor Gallery and he laughed and said, 'Oh to be a young man once again. Such adventures.'

I went back to the Grosvenor Gallery several times. There was a man at the door and it was his job to open the door and to greet each visitor with a 'good day, sir' or a 'good day, miss,' and he got to know me and he said it was so very good to see me again, but I do not think he recognised me as 'Hope'. Nor did anyone else.

By this time there were reviews in some of the arts

publications and they were not what Mr Watts had hoped for. I was thought of as having tied myself into a knot, and there were too many angles and the globe I rested on was described as a pantomime Dutch cheese; one even said that I would be none the worse for a warm bath. I felt the sting of those words, and I thought of how they must have hurt Mr Watts. And so I reported back to him that those views were not shared by the visitors to the gallery.

'There was a young woman who was suddenly pale and she dropped to the floor in a soft folding swoon and had to be revived by the application of smelling salts,' I said to Mr Watts and to his wife. 'And one gentleman stood for a half hour transfixed and he said after that he wanted to sweep the young woman with the lyre up into his arms and to make her every wish his pleasure to grant.'

Sir made a call on the gallery and he looked at only the one painting and he leaned in so close I thought he might lick the paint to see what Mr Watts' blue tastes of. He stood before the painting for so long that someone from the gallery approached him and quietly asked if he had a particular interest in the painting and if he required any assistance.

'I know the model,' Sir said to the gallery assistant. 'She is a special friend of mine and I am just looking to see that the artist has caught her right.'

Together, Sir and the gallery assistant looked again at the painting and were silent for some time before the younger man put his question to Sir: 'And has he?'

'She is really quite beautiful,' Sir said then. 'It quite takes my breath away how beautiful she is,' and with that he turned heel and left the gallery.

Sometime later I read a poem that was inspired by and built around the painting and Mr Watts presented me with a signed platinotype reproduction that I could hang on the wall of my bedroom and be like any other fashionable lady in London for they all wanted a piece of 'Hope'. But the popularity of the painting spread far beyond London and was sent across the sea to Europe and to America and to anywhere there were gentleladies and gentlemen of taste. And by degrees the critics who had thrown small stones at the picture were forced to reassess and the painting was hailed as a triumph.

'Didn't I make a promise to you, Dorothy Dene? Didn't I say that you would one day conquer the world? And lo it has come to pass for the whole wide world is taken with 'Hope' and the printing presses cannot keep up with the demand and they are saying it is my finest work and essays have been written on its significance and this is only the beginning.'

I may have blushed at this small speech from Mr Watts.

'I have another idea for a painting,' he said then.

THE WEXFORD WHALE (x)

It wasn't long ago that I went to see Mr Boland's blue whale in the Hintze Hall of the Natural History Museum. It was everything he said it'd be. The hall was like a church with its stone and stained-glass windows and all the arches and pillars and light filling the space like angels. And the blue whale skeleton like something flying and it hung in the air as if it weighed nothing at all. I approached it, like stepping towards God or royalty, and felt somehow that I should bow to its dipped head.

Then standing underneath the whale and it was as though I was inside it, swallowed like Jonah, and the whale above me was singing – Mr Boland had played the class a tape of whale song – and I thought of that sound playing through water, a vast vibration that carried the music of the blue whale for miles, hundreds of miles maybe; and it was playing through me so that I shook a little with the excitement, my legs particularly and I wanted to sit down or to weigh nothing at all and to float on the air like that blue whale skeleton was floating.

I sat down on the stone steps and twisted my body into a knot so I could look up.

I'd read somewhere that the blue whale was one of the first species to get a sort of global protection that declared we weren't allowed to kill them. That was back in 1966. Really it was all whales, though some countries still killed a small number of them. Since then the number of whales in the ocean has begun to recover but according to the science this hasn't really happened with the blue whale and no one really knows why. Mr Boland told us all, that while walking on the moon was important – and maybe one day walking on the surface of Mars too – we still had a lot to learn about what we had here on our own planet and he said how to save the blue whale from extinction was one of those things. He got really emotional when he was telling us that and I thought there was a crack in his voice and he was near to tears.

'Can you even imagine a world without blue whales in it?' he'd said.

In his classroom that day you could hear a pin drop and Kev, bent over his work as though he really loved science, looked at me like there was something to be worried about.

But Mr Boland left one important thing out when he told us about his Wexford Whale; when they moved it to the

Hintze Hall they decided to give the whale a name, something for the public to latch onto. When you give something a name that doesn't ordinarily have a name, like calling a collection of fossilised bones Lucy – and Mr Boland had a picture of Lucy on his wall – well it changes things and it somehow brings you closer to the thing named, like you know it on the level of a friend or family. And if it's a name with some meaning, that only increases the connection. The people at the museum decided to call their blue whale 'Hope', which is the name of my grandmother on my mother's side and maybe that's why, when I read the name on the plaque on the wall in the Hintze Hall, I was held there, unable to move and as close to tears as Mr Boland had been on that day in class.

Calling the whale 'Hope' was something else too, something to do with what Mr Boland had told us about saving the blue whale and our future here on earth. It was something positive also, like the scientists who had worked on the skeleton of Mr Boland's Wexford Whale had looked beyond the horizon and into the future and what they saw there was something with hope in it and not a world whose oceans were empty of blue whales.

I'd left school by the time I saw Mr Boland's blue whale skeleton in the Hintze Hall of the Natural History Museum but I still remembered his stories and I saw them a little different from when I was at school and I saw how he'd been educating us with his stories as much as he had been with the curriculum. Maybe more. And I don't know why, but I wanted to tell Mr Boland that and to say I had seen his blue whale skeleton and I'd been in the belly of the whale and I'd heard it singing deep as oceans. I decided then and there that I'd writer a letter to Mr Boland at the school.

Dear Mr Boland,

It's Devin Morrow here. I was in your class once. You taught us all sorts and I just wanted to say that I remember everything – well, mostly everything. I remember your story of the blue whale skeleton and how your father took you to see it in the Whale Hall of the Natural History Museum and you stood underneath it and looked up in wonder. I wanted to tell you that I did the same in its new home, the Hintze Hall, and I swear it was everything you said it was and maybe more. It quite took my breath away and I had to sit down on the stone steps and at the feet of a very clean and white Charles Darwin. And I thought, just for a moment, that I heard whale song, the same that you'd played for us in class.

She's called 'Hope' you know, your blue whale, and that means so much, don't you think? And I think maybe your stories were like hopeful seeds that you planted in us and I thought you should know that I love that and I will one day tell my own son or daughter – if

I am lucky enough to have a family – your story of the Wexford Whale and like that the tale will carry on maybe beyond what you ever expected from telling us it in class.

I'm at university now and studying Zoology and that I think is in part thanks to you. I have enclosed a picture of the blue whale skeleton – let's call her Hope from now on – and also a picture of a pygmy pipehorse. You said once that we still had a lot to learn about this place that we call home and the pigmy pipehorse is something just discovered and named and so I thought it might go on your wall as proof that we are learning every day.

Wishing you well

Devin

EMILIE, EMILY, E (x)

Susan Dickinson gave birth to a second child, a daughter they called Martha (Mattie for short), in 1866. But this is not to say that her marriage to Austin was happy and Emily must have hoped that one day it would be. It was also about this time that Emily's dog, Carlo, died; it was sixteen years old. Emily never took another dog into her home or her heart.

In June 1874 Emily's father suffered a stroke and died. Emily kept to her room when the simple funeral service was held in the entrance hall of the family home. The door of her room was open enough she could hear the words that were said about her father and yet not be seen.

In August 1875 Susan and Austin had a third child, a boy they called Gib; but before this event, in June 1875, Emily's mother, like her husband the year before, suffered a stroke which resulted in some paralysis and memory impairment. Emily's mother continued with her demands on Emily's finite resources for a further seven years before she passed in 1882.

It was around the time of her mother's death that Emily's brother, Austin, began an extra-marital affair with a married woman by the name of Mabel Loomis Todd, an affair that was poorly hidden from the world and must have been a source of anxiety and distress for Susan Dickinson and for Emily. This affair would last until the end of his life.

In 1883, Susan and Austin's eight-year-old son, Gib, died from typhoid.

'The dyings have been too deep for me,' wrote Emily in 1884.

In 1886 Emily died from Bright's disease, an inflammation of the tiny fibres in the kidneys. Lavinia, following her sister's instructions, destroyed all Emily's letters – that is to say, the letters she had been sent, including letters from Susan Huntington Dickinson. The poems were saved by a maid-of-all-work, Margaret Maher, who had served the family since 1869.

In 1890 a first book of Emily's poems, overseen by Mabel Loomis Todd – Austin's mistress – was published by Roberts Brothers.

*

When it arrived in the post, Martin brought it straight through to the back of the shop where I was busy making up deliveries for the boy to take out. My hand shook as I took it from him. It was wrapped plain enough, brown paper and string such as we sold in the shop, and the publisher's name was printed on the back of the small parcel. Martin fetched a knife so I might cut the string but that seemed somehow unholy. Instead, I picked at the knot until it loosened and then came away altogether. I laid it down on the deliveries table and slowly folded back the brown paper to reveal a further wrapping of soft white tissue underneath, soft and white like clouds or smoke. Inside this second wrapping was Miss Emily's book of poems.

I think I might have snatched for breath then, not realising that I'd not breathed in through all the operation of unwrapping. And hot tears stung my cheeks and I could see Martin was conflicted and did not know whether to stay or go. I waved one hand in the air by which he knew to leave me and was probably grateful to be gone from the room.

I picked Miss Emily's book up from the table. Her name was on the cover just as she had hoped one day it would be – 'Poems by Emily Dickinson'. I ran my fingers over the letters of her name and breathed deep, right to the soles of my feet. And I may have said her name then, soft like a prayer.

Then I sat in a chair at the table and just pressed the book to my heart and wept and in that weeping was so much that it is hard to explain. I wept for the joy of Miss Emily's hope coming to fruition and for Miss Emily who never would see it, unless there is a window in Heaven through which she could see me sitting holding her book clasped to me. And I wept for Miss Susan and her lost child and for lost children everywhere – I do remember Miss Emily had a fondness for children. And for the dog Carlo that, when Miss Emily was cross with the world, sometimes slept in the corner of the kitchen near to the stove. And I wept for the Master who was sometimes stern and other times soft; and for the Mistress with her brass bell. And I wept for the garden in Amherst too, Miss Emily's garden, for I knew sure as eggs or sunrises, that Miss Vinnie would not care for it as Miss Emily had and so it would soon run to overgrown, all the flowers strangled by weeds.

The delivery boy when he came in to collect his baskets of goods, whistling and quick, he saw me sitting at the table and crying over a book of poems and he stopped in his tracks and did not know if he should stay or retrace his steps and knock at the door and wait for a call to enter.

I slipped the book into the pocket of my dress, wiped my tears away against my sleeve, and pinched my cheeks pink. Then I went back to work and so the delivery boy breathed again, though he no longer whistled.

I later learned that some of the poems had been altered between Miss Emily's books that she kept locked away in her desk drawer and the poems as they appeared printed in the book. A Miss Mabel Loomis Todd – whoever that might be – had fixed the punctuation and the capitalisation and the syntax, by which is meant the arrangement of the words so they made sense and the lines was all well-formed. I was not sure what Miss Emily would have made of that, but I think she might have been pleased that her poems at least could be read – and I did read them, every one of them. Some I read out loud to Martin when we were sitting up in bed and he was leaning towards sleep but patient enough to give me his ear.

I din't always make sense of what Miss Emily wrote but I could hear her voice in what I read and that was something.

But when all's said and done, there was one poem that meant more to me than all the others and which, when I read it, brought me to tears every time, for I think it comes as near to Miss Emily as anything.

> 'Hope' is the thing with feathers –
> That perches in the soul –
> And sings the tune without the words –
> And never stops – at all –

And sweetest – in the Gale – is heard –
And sore must be the storm –
That could abash the little Bird
That kept so many warm –

I've heard it in the chilliest land –
And on the strangest Sea –
Yet – never – in Extremity,
It asked a crumb – of me.

ADA ALICE PULLEN (x)

The painting of 'Hope' that is on display at the gallery now called Tate Britain, is the second version painted by G. F. Watts and is a little darker than the first, a little gloomier. And yet when I first saw it I think I was as affected as Dorothy Dene had been when she saw the original. I was transfixed and transported all at once, and a little out of breath and unable to move. And I lost all words, just for so long as I was looking at the painting, which on that first occasion was above a half hour.

I do not believe I thought about what it meant then. The figure of the blindfold Hope just seemed so unutterably sad and alone. I did not think it an optimistic painting. But I felt it was beyond beautiful and perfect and it was the first painting I ever saw that pulled at my heart. A part of me wanted to reach out to the young woman in the painting, to take her hand and help guide her towards something better, to the fulfilment of hope perhaps.

The painting has a place in popular culture far beyond what G. F. Watts could have dreamed for the work. Its influence falls on the most privileged and the most disadvantaged in society with equal weight.

One story recounts how a woman, walking to the Thames with the intention of throwing herself into the river and drowning – her pockets heavy with cobblestones – saw a reproduction of 'Hope' on display in a shop window. She was so inspired by the image that she emptied her pockets of stones there and then and went back to her life.

The music hall star, Marie Lloyd, beset by financial difficulties at the end of her career, depressed and past her best, died in 1922. It was said that among her possessions was found a print of Watt's famous painting.

President Theodore Roosevelt had a reproduction hanging on the wall of his Summer White House at Sagamore Hill.

And in 1959 a sermon by Martin Luther King Jnr with the title 'Shattered Dreams' used 'Hope' as a symbol for its message.

It was also rumoured that Nelson Mandela had a print of the painting in his cell on Robben Island but to date this has never been confirmed.

In 1990, the young and impressionable Barack Obama attended a sermon delivered by Jeremiah Wright in which

Wright talked about the influence he had taken from Watts' painting. Obama gave a detailed account of the sermon in his book *Dreams of My Father*, and 'Hope' was a central theme of his 2006 book *The Audacity of Hope* as well as the central thrust of his successful 2008 presidential campaign.

And the painting still hangs on the wall in Tate Britain and each time that I see the work it is as though it is the first time and I come to it fresh and new and I do not speak or think or do any other thing. And like that I imagine Dorothy Dene, stepping down from the painting, placing one hand gentle on my heart, her lips to my ear, and she says, 'Just breathe'.

*

I do not know if Sir asked for it or if Mr Watts thought it a worthy gesture or maybe it was Mr Watts' wife who suggested it, for she had such a big heart; however it was, Sir was gifted the original oil sketch that was made for the painting of 'Hope'. I saw him some days, caught him adrift in his thoughts in his studio and he did not hear my footsteps or know I was by him till I spoke, and he was often looking at that oil sketch painting and looking with a fondness that I see so often in old men when they watch pretty young girls walking in the park in summer dresses. He never did say what he was searching for in the work or what he felt when he looked at the painting and I never did ask.

'I have another idea for a painting,' he said when I took his hand and he was suddenly aware of me standing beside him. And I did not roll my eyes, which is something he had taught me not to do, and I smiled and said he should show me what it was.

In 1895 he painted his last picture of me. I was curled into sleep and wearing a dress of flaming orange. He painted me beautiful, as he always did. But I noticed that he was somehow more stooped at that time and as though the weight of his years was on his shoulders and a greater burden than it had been before. And he sometimes coughed and could not so easily clear his throat. And when he got up out of a chair, the noise he made was deeper and longer; the same when he sat down in a chair. And time seemed to slow down and the air in the studio was suddenly cold.

Sometimes he did not paint and I took his arm then and we walked about his studio. He called me dear and I felt that he leaned more and more on me.

Then one day in January 1896, he was made a lord – Lord Frederic Leighton – and there was such a fuss and such a glad celebration. Sir clapped his hands and he said well to goodness but he did not know what he had done to deserve such an honour and I thought all his words were thin and misty and breathless. But he was a lord for only one day, for the next he suffered pains in his chest and it might have been his heart but he took to his bed and later died. I was with him at the end and he held my hand in his and he said my name over and over – not Dorothy Dene, but Ada Alice Pullen, and it was as though he was giving something back to me.

He left me £5000 in his will and a further £5000 was put in trust for me and my sisters, all of which was a very pretty sum indeed, a greater fortune than I'd ever thought possible and more than enough that my sisters and I would no longer have to look up at the stars, snatching at them and then keeping our fists clenched tight to the wishes we'd made; which is, I am sure, everything that my dear Lord Leighton had hoped for.

EPILOGUE – 'I HOPE…'

I hope that in reading this short book you understand it is a work of fiction and as such it runs to a different test of truth from fact.

I know, for example, that Edward (Ned) Wickham was described in his day as a compassionate man and he was, as coxswain of a lifeboat, a heroic figure; and that is not how I have shown him here.

And Dorothy Dene's relationship with the artist, Frederic Leighton, has never been confirmed as anything other than that of a devoted patron and his model – even though in a letter by a friend of Leighton's Dene is referred to as his 'wife'.

And Emily Dickinson's story, as I have told it here, is all out of order and incomplete. We do not have Susan Huntington's letters to Emily and so can only speculate as to what their relationship really was, and that speculation is based only on the letters we do have which are Emily's letters to Susan.

I know all this and hope that you take what I have written

as an acceptable truth, for it was never my intention to write biography or commentary but only to write fiction.

I hope too that you have come to this book not in search of facts but to peer inside the head of someone thinking about hope and what hope could mean and what it means for the world we live in.

If what I have written has piqued your interest and you now want the facts there are books and places I could recommend.

If the story of Hope, the blue whale and the Wexford Whale, is something you want to know more about then you could do a lot worse than start with '*Hope – the story of the blue whale*' a delightful little book by Richard Sabin and Lorraine Cornish, published by The Natural History Museum, London, 2019. It is filled up with facts.

If it is Emily Dickinson that you want to know more about, there are enough biographical works out there (though I can't help but feel that biography is at least a near cousin of fiction) but I would recommend reading '*Open Me Carefully – Emily Dickinson's Intimate Letters to Susan Huntington Dickinson*,' for a curated selection of Emily Dickinson's letters, edited by Ellen Louise Hart and Martha Nell Smith, published by Paris Press, 1998.

As for G. F. Watts' picture of 'Hope', well, there is enough on the internet to be going on with, but for a first contact might I urge you to go to Tate Britain, London, with a little time to spare, and to stand as I have sometimes stood, just in front of the painting; then just look. Maybe also listen, for people still say the same things they have always said about the painting, speaking in hushed voices as though they are talking in church. And, just in case, let me stand beside you and whisper in your ear, 'Just breathe.'

ACKNOWLEDGEMENTS

Special thanks to Patrick Jamieson who loved this book before it was even a book and who has been unwavering in his support and diligent in his editing; without Patrick's enthusiasm this would not be the book it is. Thanks to the early readers for their kind words of endorsement – James Robertson, Victoria MacKenzie, Devika Ponnambalam, Linda Cracknell – to think of such amazing writers reading my work is simply beyond words. Thanks to Anna Morrison for such a splendid cover – her work is so fabulous and I am thrilled that she agreed to do a cover for my wee book. Thanks as ever to The Demon Beaters of Lumb – they know who they are and they are wonderful. And thanks to my family who have always made room for me to be a writer.

FICTION FROM TAPROOT PRESS

Connective Tissue by Eleanor Thom (2023)

Red Star Over Hebrides by Donald S. Murray (2023)

Femke by David Cameron (2023)

The Other Side of Stone by Linda Cracknell (2021)